THE UGLY SALON
and
Other Stories

by
Garrett Murphy

*Murphy*Read

Previous Publications

"The Story of Little Awmie" and "Sisters Yabarre!" appeared in my self-published chapbook *Check Please Don't* (2013).

"Thy Love Vamp" appeared in my self-published chapbook *You Can't Be a Hero in Your Dreams* (2010).

"Marybel After the Genocide" first appeared in my collection *None Dare Call it Making Sense in An American Lesson* (Dreamsmith Ink, 2001), and subsequently in two of my other collections: *Call 9-11 and Mister Punch* (Beatitude Press, 2004) and the self-published *American American Style* (2012).

Note: Some previously published works may be slightly edited versions of their original publications.

Additional copies of this book can be purchased via:
https: www.createspace.com/5970834

Book design and cover illustration by the author.

ISBN-13 9781522995227
ISBN-10 1522995226

TABLE OF CONTENTS

The Ugly Salon

All right, all right...this is indeed owed...this does need to be told...so here it is...

1a. The Beginning...

The train sped along the tracks along the home stretch towards the resort town of Landvale, the home of the annual Bravefree Writing Salon Awards, in which seven-member teams of storytellers compete with each other for the Grand Prize, the top five finishing teams would compete with each other at the Landvale Pavilion for the Grand Prize and the chance to read their works before a national audience in Bravefree, where the winning team was guaranteed publication in the *Great Land Library of Storytellers*, an annual publication distributed worldwide, plus a celebrity-laden Victory Gala at a swank hotel and the privilege of having one's performance recorded for posterity (along with the option of owning one's own copy of the experience and a plaque in gold, silver or bronze frame).

Hugh Hyman sat awed at the scenery the train had passed by, with the six teammates he had managed to secure the final slot among applicants some months ago when the call had come out to join the members of a team to compete for the BWS Awards. It had tickled him beyond his imagination to have found acceptance at last after what had seemed to be a lifetime of mocking dismissal and jeers at his being too immersed in storybooks (and not just the fictional ones). What a vindication it would be to return home with a Grand Prize earned by the very thing that everyone had mocked him for. Already his team, Team LeCotton, was considered the frontrunning team, and most observers attributed it to Hyman himself, who was quick to remind them that he was a part---one-seventh---of the reason behind Team LeCotton's success. It felt good to at last believe himself to be of importance for a change; though even here he realized he was the youngest member of his team.

The members of each team (there were several of them on board) were psyching themselves up for the coming arrival. As they prepared to disembark, they were applauded by the passengers. One such team passing by was greeted with cries of *"Go Team LeCotton!"* and *"We're all for you!"* among other perks.

"Well," the team captain, an early fortyish woman with curly brown hair, beamed as the train approached the stop," here we are in Landvale! The future champs of the BWS Awards!"

"I can't say we're much too soon," remarked a petite elderly woman, the oldest member of the team. "I suspect I'm getting a *lit-tle* up there for all this gun!" She grinned wickedly and turned to her companion, a bald sixtyish man of rugged medium build.

"It won't be much longer," he replied, taking her arm in his to steady her. "The hotel's just a little ways from the station."

An interracial couple, a blond man in cowboy hat and attire (*easily six six*, Hyman observed) and an Asian woman, both late twentyish, gazed all around them at the sight of the town.

"Oh isn't it delightful, dear?" she asked her boyfriend.

"Yeah," he replied. "Our first stay in a hotel---only---"

"Yes...?"

"I never expected to share it with five others!" At that the entire team laughed.

The final team members, a thirtyish Latino and a black in his mid-twenties, both conversed.

"So what say you?" the Latino inquired of the black. "Nice-looking place, huh?"

"It is," the black answered. "I never imagined it'd be like this."

"Okay team!" the captain cried out. "We're in the town of Landvale looking at the Talco Inn. Now that we're of the express, we'll have to walk the rest of the way. But first, our announcements as we rehearsed them---*who am I? I am Cherry Le Cotton!*" She turned to the elderly woman. "And *who are you?*"

"*Katya Piskinova!*"

The companion. "*I am Arthur Oswald!*"

The blond man. "*I am Kingsley Marshall!*"

The Asian girlfriend. "*I am Akiko Harachi!*"

The Latino. "*I am Hector Franco!*"

The black man. "*I an Hugh Hyman!*"

"And *we are...?*" Cherry said.

"*We are Team LeCotton!*" they all said as one.

"This year's BWS champions," Cherry continued, "or we might not be in a position to know the reason why. Onward, team!"

And the members of Team LeCotton marched joyfully towards the Talco Inn.

That was what Hyman recalled of that moment they set foot in Landvale.

1b. At the Talco

"Good afternoon," a large-boned elegant woman of middle age smiled at the entrance to the Talco Inn. "You must be the members of Team LeCotton."

"We are," Cherry replied. "I'm the captain, Cherry LeCotton, and these are Katya Piskinova, Arthur Oswald, Kingsley Marshall, Akiko Harachi, Hector Franco, and Hugh Hyman."

"The star," the woman smiled, looking intently at Hyman. It always unnerved him considerably to be singled out, even for a positive reason, in part die to all the scapegoating he had always had to endure.

"Oh no," he said with humble haste. "I'm just one of the team, no more, no less."

"How considerate of you!" she laughed. "Bur how remiss I am---neglecting to introduce myself. I'm Siobhan Talco, the innkeeper and proprietor. I hope you all have a splendid time here."

Before long Mrs. Talco and the staff had shown the team to their rooms, three in all. One was shared by Cherry, Arthur and Katya, the second by Kingsley and Akiko, and the third by Hector and Hyman.

"Well," Hector said to Hyman as soon as they were alone in their room, "we're here at last. This your first time?"

"Yes."

"My second. Several years ago. My team then didn't even place. But this one's been lucky all along, don't you think?"

"I do," Hyman replied. "If I recall correctly, Cherry, Arthur and Katya have done this quite a bit...I believe Kingsley and Akiko, like me, are first timers.'

"Very perceptive of you," Hector chuckled. "But it won't be easy; as I said, my last team didn't even place. And--- well, Mr. Laird's an okay guy, but his assistant, Mrs. Tepa...she's a definite ice queen."

"Well, for now," Hyman said, "what interests me most is getting a chance to check the surroundings of the town of Landvale!"

1c. *Preparations for the Tournament, Mrs. Tepa and Reverend Avalon*

But in actuality there had been surprisingly little time to witness the sights of Landvale, as the schedule of the storytelling teams was quite regimented, allowing for little more than practicing and rehearsing for the upcoming faceoffs to determine which teams would make it to the finals. Everywhere around, it seemed to Hyman, some team was off in some corner rehearsing among the membership of said team, taking place in the Talco Ballroom, the largest single space in the Inn. Same with Team LeCotton, though Hyman was able to take note of the entire scene, in which he counted no fewer than two dozen teams, all huddled in respective spaces in the ballroom. He also noted, with little surprise, how predominately white the majority of the teams were---a sprinkling of Asians, Latinos, and others in some teams, a few had none at all. There were nine blacks in the entire room: himself, the all-black Team Avalon, and the tall, husky yet rather striking woman ("at least mid-fortyish," thought Hyman) at the door directing traffic among the teams in a matter-of-fact way. This was Mrs. Tepa, the "ice queen" Hector had warned him of.   He did rather uncomfortably recall his own encounter with her.

"Uh, excuse me, where does---"

"Team LeCotton meets over at the second corner," she had replied in a tone that, while not vicious, was crisply leaving little room for the slightest doubt.   And jutted her arm, manicured fingernail pointing with the harsh precision of a saber, in the direction of that second corner.

"Well…thank you."

"You're welcome," she had replied quite seriously.

Hyman had decided to get over to his team as fast as he could.

On another occasion, during a rare break in the hubbub, he encountered The Reverend Mr. Avalon, the captain of Team Avalon, tall, rugged, built like a linebacker, and with a salt-and-pepper goatee.

"*So!*" he said with such force it startled Hyman. "It's nice to see one try to make it outside…the *realm*."

Not quite getting Avalon's meaning, he replied "Well, sir, I just consider myself lucky to be here. But seeing you and your team is…heartwarming."

"But one word to the wise, young man," Avalon remarked. "Let your presence do justice to us all." He turned away without elaborating further, leaving Hyman to return to his team as the break was closing.

1d. Mr. Laird

The team's meeting with Mr. Laird, a silver-haired robust man, perhaps mid-sixties, proved the most auspicious of the meetings Hyman would recall of the introductions he would have that day of the mass readoffs, making him relieved that it was he who was in charge of the entire contest.

"Ah, Cherry," he beamed as he greeted them all individually (which awed Hyman---"he somehow seems able to do that with *all* the numerous contestants!"), "so you're back again, along with Arthur I see, and Katya too!"

"But of course," Cherry replied. "And this time I think I've got us a winning team---though I'm sure you hear that one from all the teams."

"Well, someone's going to be right about that," Laird remarked. "It could very well be you; then Arthur and Katya can have some company."

"You know that was some years ago," Arthur quipped. "And I was lucky enough to be allowed with all that talent."

"Me too," Katya added, "only mine was twenty-five years ago. I'm shocked anyone remembers."

"I don't forget easily," Laird said, "but let's see to the newcomers---" He turned to Hector. "---weren't you here last year?"

"Yes," Hector said. "This is my second."

"And with luck, far from your last. Then it must be you three," Laird said, meaning Kingsley, Akiko, and Hyman.

"That's right, sir," Kingsley replied. "Me and my woman Akiko saw Ms. LeCotton's ad and decided to see what it's like and here we are! Oh---my name's Kingsley---Kingsley Marshall."

"It's an honor to meet you, Mr. Laird," Akiko said.

"It's my honor to have you take part at my event," Laird smiled, then turned to Hyman. "And they say you are quite the literary wunderkind, Mister---?"

"Hyman. Hugh Hyman."

"Well, I'm honored to meet you---all of you! But now I'd better move on to the other teams. All I can do is wish you all luck! I'll be seeing---and hearing---you later on in the competition, and hopefully in the final five. Good luck, all of you!" And he turned and walked to greet yet another team.

"That's Godfrey Laird for you," Cherry quipped to her teammates. "Always keeps you buttered up for the cooking."

But as it turned out the day of the BWS contest, it was indeed Team LeCotton who "cooked," as in roasting away at the competition. It had been almost lickedly-split in Hyman's retrospective judgment. But he had been prepared to take part in it. The period before its commencement had been rather tense, teams rehearsing and practicing and in a few cases even arguing various points; all the while Mrs. Talco and the inn staff saw to contestants, contest coordinators, and ever-accumulating audiences gathering, conversing, indulging in refreshments and purchasing volumes of award-winning works by past winning teams and even well-known writers who had at some point taken part on the contest but had not necessarily won in it. Hyman, though fully concentrating on his own efforts along with those of his teammates, could not help but noticing two things; one being Team Avalon, as vigorously focused on its coordination with each other as every other team, and the other being Mrs. Adeline Tepa, watching over the proceedings from her place near the main entrance to the Ballroom, like a coldly efficient hawk.

Eventually the contest had commenced, each team chosen in the order of a random lottery. It was several hours of team after team reciting their works as a salon, to varying degrees of applause, Mr. Laird presided over the on mike proceedings, behind him was a group of five judges issuing scores on a point system, which, coupled with audience reactions, was used to calculate total scores; the top five finishing teams would compete with each other the following evening at the Landvale Auditorium for the Grand Prize.

About a third of the way into the tournament Team Avalon's name was called. They stepped forward to the podium, attired as members of a choir, led by Reverend Avalon, who, as the Team Captain, read first; he read a story of a person going through estrangement and exile from his group trying to make a name for himself and after many trials and errors finally returned forgiving and uncritical back to the group that had originally shinned him. Told in a strident yet compassionate and even cajoling manner, it had received extremely high response from the audience and near-unanimous scoring from the judges. Hyman, though genuinely moved by the story as well, felt a degree of irk he could not quite determine, he finally simply attributed it to competitor's skepticism. The other members of Team Avalon did not disappoint anyone; though none quite matched the evangelical energy of their captain, all scored well with audience and judges, securing the contest's highest score up to that point.

"That group's hotter than an Equatorial summer," Arthur remarked from Team LeCotton's sidelines. "Methinks they're going to be the ones to watch out for!"

"I feel sorry for the team who has to follow that," Hector added.

"Of course you realize that could well be us," Cherry said with a dash of gallows humor.

To all of Team LeCotton's relief, they were not the ones to immediately follow Team Avalon; their turn would not come until midway through the second half.

1e. Storytime by Team LeCotton

"The next team to read is Team LeCotton!" Laird called out from his podium. "The team captain, Cherry LeCotton, and Arthur Oswald, Katya Piskinova, Kingsley Marshall, Akiko Harachi, Hector Franco, and Hugh Hyman!" The applause roared as Team LeCotton stepped forward.

For Hyman the whole thing had been something of a blur, there was so much to absorb and watch out for, though he did recall bare-bones what each team member had focused on. Cherry, who read first, told what was essentially a children's story about a community of animals meeting up with a community of plants about the mutual endangerment of both by a (human) adversary and how the two groups, using their individual skills, managed to succeed in vanquishing this adversary.

Arthur's story had been about a man who was obsessed with weather all over the world who became the world's leading authority on such, and how his discoveries contribute to the averting of a calamity.

Katya's story was semi-autobiographical, concerning the trials of an urchin, the sole survivor of a family that had been slaughtered during the second World War, who had been rescued and befriended by a pack of vagrants forced to steal in order to survive, and how this particular urchin, who had gone on to become the best thief and pickpocket among them, had eventually had to learn new skills once the war had ended.

Kingsley and Akiko worked jointly, taking turns reading a fairy tale they had written together, and which had seamlessly incorporated his Midwestern roots and her Japanese ones; they even moved and spoke in ways that accentuated their physical oppositions (their being over a foot apart in height). Hyman recalled this story, topped with an unexpected announcement of their engagement, had gotten particularly high applause.

Hector had told a story about a young man's efforts to resist the allure of street life offered by two gangs in his neighborhood, and how his determination works to prevent a war between them.

To his surprise, Hyman had found even his own reading to be recalled as a blur; he did remember that he had told a story about a young man whose dreams of being an artist was met with dismissal and even scorn from family, teachers, and others who said he should be an executive, banker, lawyer, engineer, doctor, as artist was no occupation at all, just a hobby (or graffiti tagger) to be passed over as there were no arts programs to be found in the schools where he lived. But a chance meeting with a writer who recalled the arts programs offered years earlier offered the man encouragement, and even a pen-pal friendship enabling him to pursue his dream and succeed.

Hyman recalled how they had all felt relieved when their turn had finally ended. They could have left the tournament as some had done but had decided to stay until the end, in fairness to those who had followed them.

"And now," Laird had announced after the last teams had read and an intermission during which the judges had the scores among all the teams. "our judges have selected the five teams who will compete for the Grand Prize of the Bravefree Writing Salon Awards for this year." He opened the envelope and read the winning teams. The Second Runner-Up turned out to be Team Avalon; Hyman noted them jumping for joy energetically, all except Reverend Avalon, who simply stood proudly, beaming. Hyman and the rest of Team LeCotton stood nervously as Laird announced the First Runner-Up was announced, then---

"And the Frontrunner for this year's Bravefree Writing Salon Award is---*Team LeCotton!*"

Cherry squealed ecstatically and jumped up like a cheerleader; Arthur and Katya embraced each other; Akiko leaped into Kingsley's arms.

"We did it!" Hector cried out to Hyman, as the two vigorously shook hands. "We won!"

Hyman could not hide his joy and better than the others. "Yeah!" he beamed. "But that just means the other teams have to compete with each other and the winning team of that goes against us."

"Oh don't any of you dare play the wet blanket here!" Cherry said delightfully. "This team is going to Bravefree's Victory Gala!"

"Today this ballroom," Kingsley shouted, "tomorrow the Auditorium!"

"And after that," Akiko beamed, "Bravefree!"

"*BRAVEFREE!*" they all replied as one.

1f. Hyman and Reverend Avalon

As everyone was departing the ballroom after the conclusion, Adeline Tepa was handing passes to members of the top five teams who were to take part in the finals the next evening. "These are your passes into the Finals tomorrow night at the Landvale Auditorium. Keep yours with you at all times; you *will not* be allowed inside without one. A free shuttle travel will travel to and from the Auditorium every ten minutes; the Finals will start at seven p.m. tomorrow night! Repeat, *you must have your pass with you---*" As he received his pass and was about to go to his room, Hyman noticed the Reverend Mr. Avalon approaching him, a warm smile on his face, offering his hand to shake.

"Congratulations, young man!" he remarked. "You have done all of our kind proud tonight. I shall be privileged to look up to you tomorrow night."

"Well, I was just one of the team---"

"Sometimes, son, one is all that is needed."

"Well, in any case, Reverend, congratulations to your team."

"Many thanks, son," Avalon replied. "Good night." And he returned to his team; Hyman returned to his and more specifically to his room for some much-needed shuteye.

There was not much time before they would have to prepare for the next night.

1g. Team LeCotton basks in the Glow

Hyman recalled how excited the entire team still was the following afternoon about winning the lead spot in the final five (which, Cherry had informed them, meant they would be the last team to read) and how they had patted and praised each other and their performance.

"Man, we really nailed that one yesterday!" Kingsley remarked.

"You said it," Cherry replied, turning to Katya. "That was some tale you told there."

"I did say it was loosely based," Katya said.

"And that love story you and Akiko did together, King..." Cherry went on, "you two practically made those glowers bloom several times. And your *engagement---oh!* There ought to be a law against throwing that kind of loop in your team!" She turned to Hyman. "And you, Hugh...you provided us with the perfect closer! Nobody dared move during your reading."

"I was just following the rest of you," Hyman replied.

"But we couldn't have done it without *you*, Cherry;" Arthur remarked. "Your stewardship was the glue holding us together."

"Oh pshaw;" Cherry blushed, "you guys were the 'glue' I needed."

They stopped at the entrance to a large diner, above whose front windows said in enormous letters *Tripota*, and in much smaller letters below, *The All-American Diner*.

"There it is," Cherry beamed. "The world-famous Tripota All-American Diner they're always talking about."

"It looks so classy," Akiko replied.

"Maybe," Hector joshed, "some of that fame'll rub off on is."

"Well," Cherry replied, "as always, let's put it to a vote. Who wants to eat here? We've got a few hours before the Grand Finals."

Everyone's hands went up, for they too were interested in the local offerings.

"Very well, then," Cherry said. "Let's go, team!" And into Tripota, the All-American Diner they went.

1h. At the Tripota, Part I

"Well if it isn't the celebrated LeCotton team from this year's BWS Awards," the proprietor smiled a short rime after they had taken a group table and had a chance to examine the menus. "Word has it you're going to win it all."

"Please don't spread *that* word around," Cherry remarked. "We've already up to our eyes in avoidable egomania as it is, and we want to make this look fair. You're such a charmer, you probably say that to all the teams---please!"

"Okay, Cherry, I admit it," the proprietor said. "But word still has it on your prospects---" A young blonde waitress arrived at the table. "---oh, here's someone to take your orders. I'll let her take over."

"Ready to order yet?" the waitress beamed.

And that was where everything had turned for Hyman.

1i. At the Tripota, Part II

For roughly the next hour and a half after the waitress had taken their orders, he had waited patiently for his own order to arrive. Within the following half-hour six members of Team LeCotton were to receive their orders as requested, and warm appreciative gestures had been exchanged between each one and the affable waitress. Yet for some reason Hyman was given an order completely different from what he had ordered.

"*Oh!* I'm so sorry," the waitress stammered. "I don't understand how I made such a mistake... I---I'm still not quite well-versed at this. Pardon me, I'll get this solved..." And she rushed off, leaving a resigned Hyman shaking his head.

"Wonderful," he mused. "Everyone's well-served except me."

"Don't worry, Hugh," Cherry said. "It's probably just a little mistake; you see how crowded it is in here."

"Well, as they say," he agreed, "accidents will happen."

He waited some more, watching the others consume their meals. About twenty minutes later the waitress returned with a tray of food---but not the one Hyman had ordered.

"Look, I'm sorry," he said, trying not to upset her, "but this isn't it either. Let me write it down for you."

"Yes, yes," she said, her own frustration beginning to show. "I'm the one who should be sorry...I'm just not thinking clearly. Let me try again..." She rushed off.

"Poor thing," Katya murmured. "When I came here years ago I worked in a bakery, it took me so long to memorize some of the foods correctly."

"That can be hard even for native-borns," Kingsley remarked.

"*I'll bet*," Hyman replied, trying to conceal the chill in his voice.

Ten minutes later the waitress returned, an apologetic look on her face, with another tray in her hands. "I'm sorry sir, it turns out we've just run out of your selection. It was all by mistake, I assure you; someone had thought you'd already been served. We offer you this crab dish from earlier today as a replacement."

"The third time..." Hyman moaned in frustration, "the third time..."

"Take it easy, son," Arthur said.

"Just an honest mistake," Akiko added.

"But the third time...!" Hyman said, trying to stay calm. "And this is the worst; I don't even *like* crab---"

The violent explosion of metal tray full of plates, food, and utensils on the linoleum-covered floor interrupted not only his sentence, but the entire atmosphere of the diner. Shooting his head up involuntarily, Hyman's eyes froze at the enraged, pursed-lipped visage of the waitress above him. Her mouth did not stay closed long; the accented, fury-laced shriek exploding from it was of a near-sonic waved pitch almost sufficient to hurt the ears.

"*GET OUT OF HEE-RREEEE-EE-EE-EE---*"

It felt surreal to Hyman---

"*---you---*"

---only, he realized it was all *too* real.

"*---nee---*"

He steeled himself---

"*---eee---*"

---for the inevitable finale.

"*---GAH!!!*"

He sat stunned, not quite believing what had happened, yet very much aware that it had, barely registering the frantic commotion and hubbub around him. He glanced at the waitress; she stood firm, eyes scrunched shut, arms tightened and fists clenched, almost as if *she* had been the recipient of her own outburst. A couple of patrons gently came to her aid, to console her. Before Hyman could formulate a response to such a cruel irony, someone gingerly placed a hand on his shoulder.

It was the proprietor of the diner. "Uh, look, son, I think you should...depart. Wanda's had a rough start...she's new here...to this job and the country, she's still trying to get used to the...*culture*...around here. We'll be happy to have you at another time...it's not your fault...try to understand..."

As he rose to his feet Hyman looked around him. But it was not the proprietor he was looking to for a response---why had none of his teammates said anything on his behalf? Other patrons might have been forgiven their neutrality to a point, but why had the rest of Team LeCotton---Cherry, Akiko, Hector--- even Katya, or *anybody*---said nothing? Frozen in disbelief--- perhaps denial? And to his shock, he noted not a few patrons glaring at him as if *he* had caused all the trouble. "Why didn't he just take what they gave him in the first place!" he could imagine, perhaps overhear, some hiss under their breaths.

Without a word he walked slowly outside, waiting for a consolation comparable to what the waitress Wanda had gotten. Nothing. Not a word even from any of his teammates. He did not bother to wait any longer---or anymore.

As he bypassed the diner's window he thought he heard abrupt outbursts of jubilation, of a type reserved for honoring someone who had just achieved a significant rite of passage of initiation into a most valued echelon of importance. He deliberately refrained from looking back to confirm any details; he believed he'd procured all the knowledge he needed and more.

Tripota, the All-American Diner.

1j. Back at the Talco

He finally made it back to the Talco Inn, breathing a loud sigh of relief at the refuge he longed for after all that had occurred.

"Welcome back, Mr. Hyman," someone called out to him. If only no one had noticed. He whirled his head rapidly and nodded to acknowledge; he'd not even bothered to determine who had greeted him, or anyone else might have said anything. Wait until tonight---he pulled out his pass instinctively as if to show defiance---he'd show them---and everyone else! Realizing he was holding his pass in his hand, he quickly shoved it back inside his pants pocket.

"Are the others with you?" Mrs. Talco inquired.

"No…"

"Guess they'll be along shortly…?"

He had no answer, nor did he care about that or the others. He merely wanted to rush to his room and somehow managed to succeed at that, only trying hard not to reveal the anguish he was feeling. Why had nobody stood up for him, why had there been only silence from his teammates after the way that horrible waitress had treated him? Surely Hector and Akiko, at least, should have known the gravity of his expulsion from the diner? (*All-American Diner* indeed!) And why did they (or the rest of the team for that matter) appear to partake in that parody of an initiation rite of passage?

It was too painful for him to take in---everything was just so wrong now. All he wanted to do was shut it all out; if he was lucky he would wake up and discover it had merely been a nightmare, and that all was truly well after all. In any event, there was the contest tonight, and Team LeCotton was the frontrunner. Once refreshed, he would really give it his all, and vindicate himself by winning the prize they all beamed over. How can they shun the one who brought them that glory?

He plopped himself down on his bed and closed his eyes.

1k. *Seven-Fifty and Afterward*

When he next opened his eyes everything seemed eerily dim all around him, as if some peculiar eclipse had unexpectedly struck the immediate region. But surely there would have been some sort of advance notice, especially with a weather aficionado like Arthur on board. Rubbing his eyes, in part to help waken himself and in part as though they were somehow the cause of his disorientation, he had finally regained his mental equilibrium enough to determine that he was indeed in his room at the Talco Inn. On instinct he moved to the light switch and clicked it on. The look at the clock on the drawer jolted him with an explosive shock.

Seven-fifty? *Seven-fifty??? No-no-no-no-NO!!!* This was no eclipse…it was early evening---and the finals had begun nearly an hour ago! What was happening? And why had no one alerted him? Woken him up? No sign of Hector! He rocketed out of the room and frantically glanced into the other rooms, all were empty. Had they all gone to the contest finals? And why had they not alerted him? He returned to his room and rushed himself into his coat; there was no time to waste. Clicking his door shut behind him, he rushed down the hall unto the main area of the inn, where Mrs. Talco and some of the staff were tidying up.

"Oh! Mr. Hyman!" Mrs. Talco exclaimed. "You startled me a moment there."

"I---I'm sorry…but…do you know where the rest of my team are…?"

"They went at least an hour ago to the contest."

"They said you still needed to rest," one staff member added. "Which seemed strange since if I recall correctly, I thought the entire team had to be present."

The others nodded in agreement.

"I thought so too," Mrs. Talco replied. "But then I'm not fully up on recent adjustments they might have made…"

"That's *is* strange," Hyman thought but for some reason did not dare to say aloud, as he too had been under that impression, remembering the flyer Cherry had shown them on the way to the inn. Time to discern later---he had to get to the auditorium fast if Team LeCotton was to have a chance.

"Thanks very much," he said hurriedly, and bolted outside to hurry to the hotel enter. Fortunately it was not all that far away; and even more fortunate that he arrived at a shuttle stop just a minute ahead of the vehicle. Making his way to a seat in the nearly empty car, he sat nervously as the shuttle made its way to the hotel center. Though it was a rather quick ride, Hyman could not help bur feel delayed, for he realized how late it was. Please don't let them go on yet---please! It took all his effort to keep from screaming at himself for oversleeping like that. They might have already had to forfeit, and it was all his fault.

The shuttle finally arrived at the hotel center; as soon as it had stopped Hyman was already off it and rushing along the path to and through the entrance, not daring to stop until he was at the entrance of the hall where the contest was still in progress. A speaker was reporting the progress of the contest.

"Whoa there son!" a booth person at the entrance said joviantly. "You'll crash through the wall the way you're dashing like that."

"Has...has...do you know if Team LeCotton's gone up yet?"

"No, not at this time."

Hyman breathed a loud sigh of relief.

"But you'd better hurry," another booth person said, "they're about to be called up."

"You must be a big fan of theirs," the first added.

"I'm actually a member," Hyman replied, and dug into his pocket to pull out his pass.

And he froze in shock, for the pocket was empty.

Instinctively, he moved to another pocket, but pulled out only the return ticket.

And another pocket, then another...but *no pass*.

"*And now, we are about to hear from Team LeCotton!*" blared the loudspeaker.

"No!" Hyman cried out to himself, then turned frantically to the booth. "Look, I'm part of Team LeCotton, and I can't seem to find my pass...I---I...is it possible..."

"Oh, I'm sorry, mister, only people with a pass can get in through this point."

"I'm trying---I'm *trying* to find my pass---!" he panicked. "Can't I show something else---my ID---or---or some card---"

"That'd only tell us who you are," was the reply, "not whether you belong here. How do we know you're not trying to sneak in, answer *that* now!"

"Please, at least try to get a team member---they'll vouch---"

"We are still awaiting the arrival of Team LeCotton!" the loudspeaker cut in. *"We have been informed that there is a complication concerning their ability to go on! We will keep you informed of further developments!"*

1l. *Hyman vs. Team Avalon*

Before Hyman could respond, he noted the members of Team Avalon trudging out of the hall, disgusted and muttering at each other. 'They must have been eliminated," he thought, "and from their mood, rather brutally so. A shame..." Sympathetic as he felt, his main concern was his own teammates that he was letting down. He turned back to the booth.

"Look," he said desperately to the booth agents, "my team needs me; I've got to---"

"Well *well WELL!*" the voice of Team Avalon's captain boomed out. "Look who we have here---Team LeCotton's own pride and joy---the Oreo cookie big shot!"

Hyman whirled about to see they were fixed on him.

"Yes, *you*, traitor!" another screamed. "You ain't worth *SHIT!*"

"Listen," Hyman replied, "I'm sorry you didn't make it, but---"

"We don't need your sympathy Tom! You should've been with *your own damned kind!*"

"*My* kind?" Hyman exploded. "If you're an example of what---"

"*Ladies and gentlemen,*" the loudspeaker interjected, "*I am very sorry to announce that Team LeCotton has been forced to forfeit its participation in this contest, due to the unexplained absence of one of its members, Hugh Hyman. Therefore, the winner of this year's contest by default is---*"

"*No---ooo---ooo!!!!*" Hyman screamed out involuntarily and buried his face in his hands.

"*HA-A-AAAAA!*" The cackle exploded almost as one from the Team Avalon members.

"Now that's just got to be an irony!" the Reverend Avalon bellowed flippantly. "This fool here goes all white on a white team, thinking he's getting *bet-tah---*"

"*BET-TAH! BETTAH!*" the rest of the team echoed.

"---and look at him now!" the Reverend continued. "Done went and disgrace us *all* by chickening out like the tom he is! Ain't that right Tommy!"

"Or maybe he's really an Oreo?" another suggested.

"Maybe that's true," a third jeered, "the way he crumbled like a cookie just now."

"Probably like he crumbled and turned chicken on his own team."

"*A grave INJUSTICE to us all!*" the Reverend bellowed.

"His mama must've been an Oreo and his daddy a chicken, ain't that right Orchick?"

"*Leave---me---ALONE!*" Hyman exploded, having had enough.

"Hey, we finally got him clucking!"

"I SAID STOP IT!" Hyman screamed, and picked up a chair, throwing it at them. It missed them all, but the booth agents had summoned security to the area, and two of them moved towards Hyman.

"All right, mister, you'll have to---"

But Hyman, driven to a frenzy, had bolted out of the hall before the officers could reach him, the imagined and real taunts of Team Avalon pounding at him. However, the most vivid and harrowing sound he left behind came from the loudspeaker:

"It has just been announced that those members of Team LeCotton who had been ready to perform will be presented with the consolation prize of a trip to the Winners Convention in Bravefree to witness the performance of the winning team and all the other highlights. No need to let that integrity and effort go to naught because of one member's negligence."

1m. Hyman's Moments of Truth Continue…

Hyman had absolutely no idea, and far less to care, about which direction of what street he trudged upon or how long he had traveled; everything was incredibly surreal to him, like a dream from which he could not wake from despite all the standard efforts to do so that emerged as soon as one realized at that crucial moment as one began to wake. He may or may not have been lost physically, but that mattered least of all to him, for he was lost in every other way---for him, the contest was very much over; equally so for Team LeCotton, and all because of him; his reputation was by far the most irrevocably lost---he was now forever tarred as a deserter, destined to be as gone as the daylight now was. The night was starless, only the lights of the buildings around him prevented a pitch blackness without to match the pitch blackness within his heart---a darkness to which he now felt himself sentenced for life. What on earth had happened to his pass? At least the others would be able to *see* Bravefree if only as spectators; *he* quite likely never would, assuming he was even *allowed* there after his disgrace. *A traitor not worth SHIT!* as Team Avalon had put it, *Going all white and getting BET-TAH and then disgrace us ALL!* He sure proved them right, not just them but all of blood and not who had brusquely admonished him to "get that longhead dream out of your head and get REAL!" Well, if this was "real," he liked the dream better...only now the dream was shattered and he had nothing but "real" to keep him down. All that mattered to him now was trying to find some realization of the impossible goals of safety and warmth.

He found himself in shock when he turned to pay attention to his surroundings, for he realized he was practically facing the Laird building---where Mr. Laird, the sponsor of the contest, was headquartered. How had he managed to find his way there? Instinct? No matter, he had come across a most unexpected out---a vindication of sorts. If he could convince Mr. Laird of what had occurred, maybe---just maybe he could undo this, perhaps even get Team LeCotton back in the contest. What a save that would be. He moved cautiously to the doors of the building until he was able to place his hands upon them. To his surprise, they opened. He looked around, stepped inside, and ventured through the lobby to where the elevators were. Looking at the directory, he found Mr. Laird's offices, and pressed the button for the elevator.   An elevator opened soon afterwards, Hyman stepped inside, pressed the button, the doors closed, and Hyman felt himself ascending towards some moment of truth. Still surreal, but now there was a hope, albeit slim, for some sort of salvation which lay ahead.

The elevator door opened, and Hyman stepped off, to find himself in a small hallway facing two large oak doors, one with a golden place reading *Godfrey Laird, Chief Executive Officer* and below it in slightly smaller letters, *Adeline Tepa, Executive Secretary*. "Swell," he thought glumly, dreading the thought of possibly facing that iceberg Mrs. Tepa. But even if she was there, Mr. Laird could overrule her.

With a strength that would have stunned him had he been in any frame of mind to reflect on it, he pushed the doors open, not bothering to consider why anything had been open at this hour, why there had been no security guard in sight, or how easily he had gotten by; no, he had enough to ruin many a fruitful night from now on, not the least of which was the now-smashed dream of being part of the Salon of the Year at Bravefree, and the fact that it had been his fault. How could he have lost the pass? *How?* He *had* kept it on him---

Tepa stood before him, in front of her desk. "Mister Hyman! What are *you* doing here? This *is* well past hours."

At her full height, he realized she was almost as tall as himself (and, counting her stiletto heels, might have been taller). As always when he'd seen her, she was impeccably attired as an executive secretary ("---or maybe a church lady?" he unexpectedly thought) would be, and with as calculating a glare. Luck holding up *very* well tonight; she would be the first person he ran into. And yet now that he did get a full look at her, he could not help but realize how striking she was; no ingénue, but quite alluring in a mature way; a little bit husky but still shapely in an athletic way. He breathed in to brace himself.

"I've got to see him..." He almost believed he was somehow outside his body, observing himself and his actions. "I've got to see Mr. Laird---"

"I'm afraid that's not possible---"

"Then *make it possible!*" he snapped with a desperate ferocity he did not recognize, and began towards the closed doors on the other side of the office, but Tepa suddenly intercepted him.

"I said *you cannot see him,*" she replied, deftly tripping him up, sending them both to the carpeted floor, "---and I mean *you---can---not---see---him!*"

"I've got to," Hyman said, as much a cry as an enraged rant, trying to rush to his feet. "I've got to speak to him---!"

"It's no use doing that now," she remarked, refusing to let him loose or up. Hyman, in a furious and despondent frenzy, turned on her, and the two of them rolled, tumbled and grappled against each other on the floor; Hyman fighting hard to free himself from Tepa's grip but unable to shake her loose; she stayed right on him, holding him close almost like a bear hug and using nearly everything from head to toe to have to fend off in some way. Their faces nearly touched each other; his desperate and anguished; hers determined and serious yet not without sympathy. Their battle had two other fronts--- his hand instinctively outstretched towards Mr. Laird's office was met and countered by her fingers gripping it; and whenever he attempted to gain a toehold to enable him to rise or at least advance toward that office she managed to dislodge his foot with her own. And while he did gain the upper hand for a moment or two, she snatched it right back inevitably. He never got any closer to Mr. Laird's office than he had been when Tepa had grabbed him; she was like a mother lion protecting her cub or hearth. And yet as he quixotically trued to reach those doors anyway, hoping for the Hail Mary that would save him and his good name despite his executive secretary's blocking him at every turn. This woman, stylishly attired yet proving a most tenacious fighter nonetheless; he realized he was fighting almost as ferociously as with her an urge to shift to a playful scuffle instead; both efforts ultimately proved futile. He thought for a time he could hear her whisper in his ear; he tried not to believe it, he needed to reach Laird, he *had* to---to free himself of Mrs. Tepa---

A violent series of knocks broke his train of thought. He thought he heard Tepa gasp softly. Before he could make a sound himself, she suddenly clasped a hand over his mouth, while continuing to wrap herself around him.

"Mrs. Tepa! Mrs. Tepa! Is everything all right?"

"Yes---yes, it's all right...!" she said a little hastily, pressing Hyman's mouth a little to warn him not to try to speak. Hyman got the message, though at this point it had not been necessary, for he was none too eager to face security at all. But he then realized another message---a sensation on his calf. Again, it was Tepa; she was softly (and truth be told, with occasional doses of playful tease) caressing his leg, using the same foot that had held his own at bay moments earlier, as though to reassure him that she was really an ally rather than adversary. It then dawned on him that she had been trying to convince him of that all along but he had been too busy trying to resist her to realize it until now.

"Some items just fell off the shelves," she continued to the guards. "I've been picking them up, but another one fell again. You know how things sometimes go in dominoes."

"Well, yes...you sure you don't need any help?"

"Positive. Continue with your rounds. I'll contact you if I need help."

"Very well, Mrs. Tepa. Sorry to have interrupted you."

"No problem."

Hyman heard two sets of heavy footfalls fade from earshot. Tepa relaxed her grip on his mouth, though she still held him tightly around his waist. He could feel her breathing relax.

"Well that was close," she remarked. "That would have spoiled all the fun. You finally got my message too." She kicked his leg slightly in jest.

"*Fun---?*" he grumbled incredulously as he sat up.

"It got everything out of your system, didn't it?"

"It might have if you'd let me see Mr. Laird."

"As I said before, that's not possible…because he's not here, and you can't wait in his office. It's set up with an alarm system so if you had tried to enter, security would have been alerted and you'd have been in handcuffs and a cell instead of in my embrace.'

"Nothing seemed to happen when I entered *this* office."

"It would have, dear, had I not turned mine off, and I had my reasons for that."

"For me, no doubt."

"True," she replied with a bemusement that surprised Hyman. But he was still too upset to give it much thought.

"Well," he said with angry resignation, "I suppose you've got what you wanted, namely the chance to give me your own frosty sendoff. I do hope you enjoy savoring that victory." With disgust he moved to rise, but without warning Tepa threw herself onto him, sending him down on his back, and swiftly straddled him schoolgirl style.

"That's *not* what I wanted at all, son," she replied in a serious tone. "I *did* want you to come here, but certainly not for any 'frosty sendoff---' your teammates, I'd presume, have already given you that. Me---I just want to know you."

"*Know me?*'

"That's right." She moved her face close to his, almost touching it; her tone remained very serious, but it was tempered with compassion. "I want to know your story, Hugh Hyman…what makes you tick up 'till now. You owe me quite a bit, son…lying to any form of security, even to protect one far

34

more deserving of a storytelling prize than being a target for their macho games, is very serious business, and I do intend to call in that debt. In return I'll see to it that nobody'll hurt you any more tonight."

"All right," Hyman conceded, "touché on that You've got me. But what---"

"You heard me," she remarked. "Just tell a story...any genre or type will do, though I'd rather hear yours. But in any event, *I'm not letting you go until you do.* I *am* head lioness here and potential executioner, not to mention the former girl's wrestling champ at my high school---don't ask how long ago that was---so whether you channel Scheherazade, a sparring partner or a prey cub, I suggest you start telling." She tightened her hold momentarily to warn that she meant business. Hyman felt the movement of her body pressed atop his; he felt he could feel her every muscle keeping him at bay, yet something about her demeanor, indeed throughout everything, informed him that although she *did* mean business, she was neither trying to cow, hurt or humiliate him---more like a form of maternal (or even--- *loving?*) protection. (*Is this woman in---heat?*) Whether she was or not, he did feel obliged to trust her, he *had* to at this point, especially considering that she *was* providing precisely what he had most sought on the way here.

"All right, all right...this is indeed owed...this does need to be told...so here it is..." he began.

2. *Return to the Beginning and the Remainder...*

"That's...the story, Mrs. Tepa," Hyman sighed in resignation, not even trying to look up at her for any sign of approval. Tepa stared down at him attentively, and all was briefly silent. That was no true matter to Hyman; deep down he wanted to simply lay there under her warm protection.

"That sounds more like an autobiography than a story, son," she finally replied with a mild flippancy, "but it does answer a lot of what I've been wondering all along, so you pass. Congratulations!" And she kissed him gently on the cheek.

"*Whoo-pee*," he simpered.

"I *do* mean that, dear," she replied warmly. "Since you leveled with me, I think I've a duty to level with you, starting with this." She shifted her body, easing herself upwards, parts of her body rubbing against his in the process, suggesting to Hyman that she had been no less reluctant to break the contact than he had been. He made no effort to rise himself; he simply lay as he was, unable to summon the will to move. He heard Tepa click on something from the desk above.

It was an answering machine.

"*Hello, Mrs. Tepa…Mrs. Talco at the Talco Inn. I'm so sorry to bother you at this hour, and I'm afraid it's too late to affect the contest in any way, but I hope you receive this message. Mr. Hugh Hyman, who was supposed to be there as part of Team LeCotton, had been left behind when the others had left for the competition, but when he realized they were gone he was in shock, and he rushed off to join them. But as my clean-up crew was emptying the garbage they found a torn-up pass to the event. We hastily taped together the pass and I rushed to get it to Mr. Hyman, but we were too late. Someone had said that Mr. Hyman had indeed arrived but, as he had no pass, was not allowed in, and at that moment it was announced that his team had forfeited die to his absence and another team had won instead. After a brief altercation with another team and security Mr. Hyman fled and has not been seen since. Mrs. Tepa, I must inform you of this: When he retired to his room, Mr. Hyman* did *have his pass on him, I and two of my staff had seen it ourselves. Perhaps it's the cop's widow in me, but the only way it could have been lost is if someone had deliberately pick pocketed it off him while he was asleep. The only ones who had come by during that time were Miss LeCotton and Mrs.*

36

Piskinova, the latter of whom did mention a history of having been a pickpocket during the war. I realize I've no way to prove my suspicions, but I'd hazard a guess that that was what happened. I realize I'm imposing, Mrs. Tepa, but if you do see Mr. Hyman, please have him contact the Inn---"

Tepa clicked off the machine and turned to Hyman, who had partially sat up, shaking in anguish and sounding as if he were valiantly resisting the impulse to break into tears. Almost infantilely, he had clasped her ankle, head resting on her foot as if they were a lifeline between him and a plunge to oblivion. She did not try to break his hold, instead looking sympathetically upon him.

"I'm so sorry, Hugh," was all she could say at that moment.

"Maybe...maybe it would have been better if you'd let security have me..." he choked after a few moments of silence.

"And pass up the golden opportunity to get up close and personal with the most gifted storyteller this year?" She finally bent down and gently pulled him up. "Get up already; this's no way for a talent like you to look!" Her tone was a joshing one, but Hyman remained downbeat.

"Some gift," he said, "thrown to you and nobody else. Might as well go down as the most gifted screwer of his team's prospects."

"Look at me, Hugh Hyman," she remarked in a tone that threatened to become a command. Hyman snapped to attention involuntarily. *"You,* mister, did *not* screw your team---*they* screwed *you---"* Her tone softened a little. "---though personally I feel they really screwed themselves, even if they have been invited to Bravefree as consolation."

"Why...why?" he said brokenly, as though to an indifferent wind.

"From what you said," Tepa replied, "I'd say it was when you asserted yourself in that diner. You made clear you weren't just going to take what they tossed your way, to be a compliant eager-to-please boy, and that, to put it mildly, made them nervous. So they decided to get rid of you, even knowing that it meant forfeiting the contest. Better, to them, to go down in defeat than to owe their success to a black man---especially one who was younger than they---and you *were* their ticket to that success, Hugh, I'm not kidding about that. I knew it, so did Mrs. Talco, Team Avalon, that was why they were so hostile to you---and so did Mr. Laird; he was so enraged when he was made aware of what had occurred that I was afraid some ogre had possessed him!

"But it did work out quite nicely for Team LeCotton---it got them a sympathy image along with that consolation prize trip to the Victory Gala, with all the perks and trimmings. Which in a way is a victory, since now they don't have to throw something together to perform. No wonder Mr. Laird was so incensed---it was a perfect scam."

"But I made no scene," Hyman said incredulously. "I *was* courteous..."

"That's the trouble with being black and American, dear," Tepa replied. "Sometimes we can be a perceived threat simply by existing and not being a sponge."

"So now I exist as a disgraced would-be storyteller notorious for letting my team down when they needed me. And back to the days of being the overage mascot ne'er-do-well I was designated to be by all the perfect elders, namely practically everyone! The Cousin Arthur of all I'm allowed to be---and I do *not* mean Arthur Oswald!"

"I'll let you in on a snippet of my own, Hugh...I know quite well how that feels. I grew up with an older sister who was not only a beauty queen but also the class valedictorian;

talk about measuring up. The Marcia to my Jan, though in my case Cindy would've been a more exact analog. Since star was closed to me, I chose tomboy, the alternative route to being looked up to 'till I found my talent. Count your blessings, Hugh, you're at a stage it took me years, along with an early marriage and almost as early widowhood, to reach."

"I certainly don't feel blessed, Mrs. Tepa," Hyman said sadly. "You do make sense...but I still feel so disgraceful about letting down my---"

"*They* let *you* down, son," Tepa reminded him. "They, not you, are disgraced, and most of us are already on your side, probably more than you may realize, and Mr. Laird is among them. He's in Bravefree preparing for the Victory Gala and--- and this is why he's so angry---he has to prepare a speech to introduce Team LeCotton there; that's why he isn't here. I had come here to prepare for the next morning and noted the machine light blinking, turned on the playback button and heard Mrs. Talco's message. I had just finished hearing it when I spotted you approaching, and it took some frantic rush doing to get all the monitors to look the other way at crucial moments, *and* deactivate my own alarms."

"So you did it all for me," Hyman said sarcastically. "I don't mean to sound ungrateful, Mrs. Tepa, but---"

"Not *quite* all for you," she said. "I did mention I had reasons of my own...*which reminds me*---" Her words took on a mock-accusatory tone. "That implication of me being in heat was rather sneaky of you."

"I'm---sorry---I'm afraid that just---came out..."

"Don't be sorry," she reassured him. "I do know such feelings can occur in the...*heat*...of the moment, to *any* of us. In any event, perhaps you should see that as, say, a positive screw, dry as it was, to balance all the negative ones you got today. Or simply regard it as a one-night stand."

"Oh…my…" Hyman gasped, not finishing, as though realizing something.

"I'm not the ice queen everyone thinks I am, I'm afraid," she continued. She sat down on her desk, crossing her legs. "But it is a useful facade, given my position here. After my husband was killed and I was…stranded here, they offered me a position here as what they'd call consolation or even color-blindness. Having no real choice, I accepted and, over the years developed the role of ice-queen no-nonsense businesswoman not to be trifled with, becoming so good at what they expected me to be even the police won't lightly cross me, eventually becoming the official second-in-command, and head lioness---which in the wild is like the queen in chess."

"The most powerful piece," Hyman replied.

"Indeed," she said in mock-coquettishness. "Which in turn enables me to adopt a secondary role…you've heard of *The Spook Who Sat by the Door*?"

"Yes…" Hyman realized the gravity behind

"Well, I happen to be a spook as well…not quite as vital in the scheme of things as that protagonist…but essentially to watch over young authors, particularly though not exclusively the black ones---and do what I can to protect them from the elements that spill out over these parts, and which you got a taste of. But it's a lonely crusade, and…I guess partly because it's a milestone anniversary of my husband's death, and partly because you were a compelling storyteller, the most dangerous---and endangered type---from what I learned from Mrs. Talco's message…I took a more intimate action with you than I normally would, Hugh---far more intimate than I'd intended."

"Which had been to simply sit me down and talk it out with me."

"Definitely. But you were much more frenzied than I'd expected and, seeing me as yet another threat, started fighting me, which threw me off my game plan and…well, you can obviously guess how one thing led to another---you did catch all my gestures in your story rather accurately. I *was* turned in by you, Hugh; that tussle offered me a release, a chance at intimacy and ecstasy I'd not had since my marriage, a chance to once again feel a man wriggle under me, to feel my power…in school I had to do with other girls, but it was always the boys I craved, either squelching their machismo or arousing their desire." She folded her arms, assuming her matter-of-fact pose. "Well, Mr. Hyman, there you are. Nice material you've got for some tabloid."

"No, Mrs. Tepa---" Hyman began, actually relieved by her revelation. "This is definitely staying between us. I'm not at all into exposes---"

"One more thing," she interrupted, returning to her feet. "Call me Adeline…that's my first name…and my penultimate command to you."

"So what's the last one---Adeline?"

"To go home, Hugh," she replied. "There's really nothing more you can do here…save stopping over at the Talco Inn to let them know you're okay. Yes, I could call them and tell them so, but I think they'd rather hear it from you. Besides---" She looked out the window. "---it's dawn already! How time did fly! In other words, I'll need to change in preparation for the new day after mussing this attire up. You *do* have a return ticket home, don't you?"

"Yes, they didn't swipe that."

"Good. Come here a moment, will you."

Hyman did so, and Tepa embraced him with a force as powerful as her restraint of him had been. "I'll let you in on something: in all the years I've been at this job, I've seen and encountered many writers, scribes, and storytellers who'd made it big, and others who went on to make it big, and what they all had in common was---none of them made it big by winning this contest. A few had taken part in the contest, but none of them had actually won. A few words to the wise, and an admittedly long-winded way of admonishing you to *not give up your writing*…you've too important a talent and potential to let it go to waste because of one mishap. Promise?"

"I promise."

She released him and led him to another door. "This is a secret exit used for when Mr. Laird doesn't wish to be bothered with questions…or security. Take care of yourself, Hugh…I'll do whatever I can to clear your name. Oh…I just realized---do you wish me to say anything to Team Avalon? On your behalf, I mean."

"I honestly don't care one way or the other. I did say, after all, I don't like crab."

"Point taken."

"Anyway, thanks…for everything, Mrs---uh---*Adeline*. I mean that." And he entered the passageway, through which, somewhat sooner than he'd expected, he found himself exiting out into the slightly breezy morning air. Then, after looking about him in reflexive wariness, he started off to the Talco Inn.

He stood at the Inn's entrance, deliberately took his time steeling and psyching himself for what he feared might happen. Only what he believed was his obligation and debt to Tepa prevented him from simply bypassing the facility and walking away and the heck with everything. Taking a deep breath, he crept to the door and, overcautiously, as if expecting trouble, opened it.

"Mr. Hyman!" a guard exclaimed. "Thank goodness you've shown up. Mrs. Talco was worried about you. Wait here while I get her."

Hyman stood still as the guard moved to an intercom. Though signs in the lobby invited all to sit and relax, he did not feel comfortable in doing either; he was still jumpy with apprehension. A side effect of all that had happened over the last 24 hours, he surmised.

Mrs. Talco arrived within a minute. Hyman noted she was carrying an envelope and a couple of suitcases---his suitcases---with her. "Good morning, Mr. Hyman." ("Quite hospitable," Hyman noted, as though a bit surprised by that.) "You don't realize how relieved we are to hear from you."

"Yes," he replied. "I ran into Mrs. Tepa and she informed me of your message."

"Good...very good," Mrs. Talco said. "That means I can offer amends of my own. This...is for you." She raised her envelope hand and placed the envelope in his. "It's your share of the hotel fee. In light of all that's happened, we cannot in good faith accept your part of the payment. I guess you can consider that a consolation prize of sorts."

"I...don't know what to say..." Hyman remarked, accepting the envelope with slight reluctance, as he noted the insistence in her eyes. "I almost feel I'm bilking you."

"Nonsense," Mrs. Talco said in a gentle yet firm tone. "If anything you were the one who was bilked, and I don't feel right accepting payment from anyone so they can then be robbed. Guess that comes from being a cop's widow. In any case, this'll hopefully keep you from bearing any animosity towards us in any way."

Hyman had never held the Inn or Mrs. Talco culpable in what had happened to him and was about to say so when something in Mrs Talco's eyes warned him that she had already deduced that fact---some time ago. "Another thing coming from a cop's widow," he thought to himself.

Something came to his mind. "Uh, Mrs. Talco…this'll sound strange, I think…but can I have one last look at…our rooms…?"

Mrs. Talco turned to a maid. "Has work began on the new patron's room?"

"We were just about to start in a few minutes," the maid replied.

"Okay, I think it can wait a little longer…" She turned back to Hyman. "Let's have that last look, shall we?"

"Of course," she said to Hyman as they passed and glanced at the rooms he and Team LeCotton had stayed in, "you know that the rest of them checked out early this morning to travel to Bravefree. Your belongings are the only ones left."

Hyman examined the three rooms thoroughly, they now appeared quite vacant as if they had never been resided or slept on. He stood still silently through each room, as though offering each a moment or two of silence. As soon as he was done with all three rooms he turned to Mrs. Talco. Then another thought hit him.

"Did---did Team Avalon leave already?"

"Yes, at the crack of dawn. They're probably almost halfway home by now. One can't really blame them for wanting out so fast…you may be aware that they were the first to be eliminated, and from what I was told, quite humiliatingly so."

Hyman couldn't help breathing a loud sigh of relief. One potential issue of contention removed from the world of his problems.

"*Well---*" he began, but noting the near-smirk his tone was developing, stopped himself and shifted his focus back to her gestures. "---I…thank you very much, Mrs. Talco. I'd best get to the station; I don't wish to miss my train."

"No, of course not," she replied. "If you should come out here again, Mr. Hyman, please consider staying here again. We'd be happy to accommodate you---who knows, perhaps you'll even be a famous writer by then."

"Maybe." (*Another* vote of confidence?) "Either way, I will consider it. Good day, Mrs. Talco."

"Good day to you, Mr. Hyman. May you have a pleasant trip home."

All the way to the station he wracked his brain over another question: Should he follow the others to Bravefree, confront and perhaps expose them---perhaps causing a scene or scandal? (Which of course could mean a series of ramifications he had no certainty that he could handle?) Or follow Adeline's advice and continue the battle at another time, in another way yet to be discovered? (Or, for that matter, emulate Reverend Avalon's protagonist?) In actuality though he realized he had had no trouble making a choice. He moved quickly towards the station.

He arrived there several minutes ahead of the train. As it arrived and he stepped on board he looked back at the town of Landvale, the town where he had dreamed of victorious glory and ended up with loss, betrayal and notoriety, and, despite Adeline's promises of remedying that little mess, he knew that would always stay within his psyche for life.

And yet, seated aboard as the train sped on its way to his home he somehow knew that he would indeed return there despite everything and even travel to Bravefree---as the success whose credit for achievement would never go to Team LeCotton. He realized that would be his best revenge, and justice.

And that is a modification of one of the stories he would tell years later after he had indeed become a remarkably successful writer. The names of those he remembered and respected most fondly from that time were changed out of respect for said persons.

And as for the rest, such as Team Avalon and the rest of Team LeCotton and even the waitress Wanda…well, those names were substituted because, you see, Hugh Hyman had long since forgotten or cared about remembering those.

The Story of Little Awmie

This is the tale of a lad named Awmie. But to be honest, it's a bit misleading to call Awmie a lad, for in truth dear Awmie was an adult like his teachers. Now you may have heard of beings in certain mythological or magical tales known to some as sprites, at least some of whom were actually adults who chose to behave like, well, rather spoiled children. That was essentially what Awmie was, only without the magical or mythological context. To paraphrase Dr. Seuss, there was no explaining the reason; it might have been that Awmie, being the automatic prize student of the institution he was in, was given all kinds of allowances and privileges unavailable to most others; only a select and chosen few could ever obtain such leeway.

Yet Awmie for some reason was the one who always had to be restrained, contained, and corrected by the teachers, as the other students, well aware of their lowlier positions within the institution, were able to get around their lesser positions by simply playing on Awmie's vanity and avoiding giving their teachers any cause for their own restraint---which turned out to be surprisingly easy.

There was the time when some of the other students had sneaked outside the school to look at the city libraries and had discovered books that were about famous and should-have-been famous heroes and heroines of their own varied heritages and cultures and languages---not like the homogenous misinterpretations common in the institution's library.

"What an eyepopping time I had," one said, "learning all that about my religion!"

"Gee," another said, "and I thought all there was to my heritage was evil and illiteracy!"

"And that fella I read of," said a third. "Who'd've thought he'd accomplish so much!"

"Yeah, it's so cool to know you too might be of importance."

"Sure don't say that in this place's deadbeat library."

"Or Dopey Doodlemax's fogy lily classes."

"You take that back!" Awmie (who happened to revere the classes) burst in.

"Oh boy it's that Awmie again," said one.

"Prob'ly mighty sore 'cause we're not talking about *his* heroes."

"Or *ze*-roes."

"Our facility's texts are *NOT* zeroes!" Awmie burst out. "Our school offers GOOD texts, teaching GOOD solid values. Professor Doodlemax wouldn't be recommending them if it wasn't the best of our knowledge!"

"Look, Awmie, just because you're the teacher's pet and prize student, there's no need for you to vent all over the place."

"I'll vent all over YOU!" Awmie exploded. "Like *THIS!*" He swung at them, again and yet again, wildly as the others simply leaned back from him.

"Stand still!" he growled. *"HOLD STIL-L-L-L!!!"*

"Yeah, sure," was the reply as they ducked and dodged in ways that suggested they believed poor Awmie's outburst to be taken less than seriously.

But Professor Doodlemax took it quite seriously. He rushed to the scene. "HEY! Break it up, boys!" (His voice was a cross between Roger Ramjet and Max Headroom.) He snatched up Awmie and held him as one would an unruly charge. "H-H-H-H-H-Hold it boys!"

"Lemme at 'em *LEMME AT 'EM!*" Awmie cried. "I'll---"

"Now-now-now Awmie," Doodlemax replied as he carried the squirming child-man off, "we all-all-all admire

50

your presence, and we know you're very important to us, but-but-but you are the one misbehaving, you're the one who's creating a scene-scene-scene, so we'll have to give you a time-time-time-time out until you've come to your senses."

"*Lemme go... len-ne go---LEN-NE GO-O-O-O-O-O!!!!!*" whimpered poor Awmie.

"Sorry son, no can do," Doodlemax replied as he led Awmie off, away from the other students who watched him being carried away and struggling to suppress a laugh or snicker.

Now there were a group of students of the institution who engaged in using some very unique code languages (which were *not* of the profane type, let's make that quite clear!) with each other, which of course infuriated young Awmie. "English is the sole way to communicate that's all!" he boasted.

"Really Awmie?" they smiled. "Hey fellas, let's discuss the matter and see if he makes sense." And they did so---in one of their secret little lingos, pointing in his direction every now and then.

Poor Awmie didn't like that one bit no he didn't---he knew what was best; how dare they talk their talk! And soon he assumed they were talking about *him* (as he believed he was the only thing worth discussing). And he did not like to be discussed behind his back, especially in a language he didn't understand.

"*Mwheeeeleeeemeememeemeeemee...*"

"*SHUT UHN-N-N-N-NNNNN!!!*" Awmie yelled.

"*Wwwheeemuleeeleeemweeeewaeeeemueeee...*"

"*SHUT UHN-N-N-N-NNNNN!!!*"

"*Weeeemuweewhueeewufeeeeevaeeeeeaeeeeewueeeeeeee...*"

"*SHUT----UNNNNNNNNNNNNNN!!!*" And he stomped and stamped himself into a noisy and disruptive frenzy, which of course brought out all the participants in a teacher's discussion, led by the headmaster, Principal Minimal, who snatched him up by the collar of his shirt and marched him off.

"That's quite enough out of you, young man," the principal lectured the hapless Awmie. "Although you are our favorite charge, you'll just have to learn some discipline!"

"Leggo!" Awmie sobbed. "Leggo you!"

"I am not a you, good Awmie. I am a principal--- Principal Minimal to you, and you are a most naughty boy we are regrettably forced to put in detention."

And the other students looked on at this scene, after which (and after the other teachers had returned to their discussion) they resumed their conversation in their own respective tongues.

Now of course no co-ed institution worth its salt would be without issues concerning the…female persuasion, and so it was with this one as well; when there was a recent get-together between the boys and the girls, and of course you guessed it! Awmie, believing himself to be quite the ladies man (or girl's boy as the case may be), was sure he would be invited in as soon as he arrived. So that night where the event was being held he rushed to the door, sure to be invited inside, and knocked on it.

"Who is it?"

"It's me, Awmie, come to conquer!"

A snicker followed, and no more.

"*Hey!*" Awmie bellowed. "I'm supposed to be let in here with the girls and the food and dance are ALL FOR ME!"

More snickers followed, much to Awmie's indignation. He banged on the door. "Hey! Let me in!"

Silence.

"*LET ME IN-N-N-N-N-N!!!*" he wailed, banging rapidly and now kicking the door. *"LET ME IN-N-N-N-N-N!!! LET ME IN! LET ME IN LET ME IN LEMME INNNNNNNNNNNNNNNNNNNN!!!!!!!!*"

(Now it must be noted that Awmie could have simply opened the door and let himself inside as everyone else had, but despite knowing that, he had expected to have someone open it for him anyway, for, after all, was *he* not the favored one of them all?)

But don't you worry, for you see, Awmie did end up receiving someone of the female persuasion, or rather, she received him, as it was the teacher Miss Tee, Amazonian of build and sunny of face, complexion, and demeanor, who grabbed him and held him to her bosom.

"Awwww you poor dear Awmie," she said endearingly, "you obviously don't understand why nobody's letting you in there. We know you are the apple of all our eyes but you really can't go around banging and kicking and throwing all kinds of tantrums can you?"

"*Lemme go...lem-me go...LEMME GOO-O-O-O-O!*" Awmie whimpered, now really struggling ferociously, for this was, after all, a female, but all he managed to do was send them both tumbling to the ground---and she still held him tightly.

"Awmie, this will not do," she said, undaunted, as she maneuvered him into her lap, maintaining her viselike hold on him. "We'll just have to ground you for a little while."

"*Leggo...leggo...LAAGO---LAAAAGO!!*" he wailed, squirming as hard as he can, but with no success.

"Hush now, dear Awmie," Miss Tee murmured.

From inside the room where the get-together was held, some apparently had witnessed the scene, for guffawing sounds could be faintly heard.

Now after all the troubles poor Awmie had had it was decreed at that discussion that there should be something dedicated to the institution's prize student. So after much discussion over here and over there a song was dedicated to the lad by the a cappella vocal group who had somehow survived the axes that Awmie had been spared. That song went as follows:

NAH-NAH-NAH-NAH-NAH
NAH-NAH-NAH-NAH-NAH
NAH-NAH-NAH-NAH-NAH
NAH-NAH-NAH-NAH-NAH!

Little Aw-mie thinks that he's a great big he-ro.
NAH-NAH-NAH-NAH-NAH
NAH-NAH-NAH-NAH-NAH
Poor boy didn't know that he's really a big ze-ro.
NAH-NAH-NAH-NAH-NAH
NAH-NAH-NAH-NAH-NAH
Shoulda known he should've tried for some great deal-o
Instead of blowing off like the Emperor Ne-ro.
Little Aw-mie thinks that he's a great big he-ro.
NAH-NAH-NAH-NAH-NAH   (Hold it boys!)
NAH-NAH-NAH-NAH-NAH   (Huh-huh-huh-hold it boys!)

Big bad Awmie thought he had the big ap-pe-al.
NAH-NAH-NAH-NAH-NAH
NAH-NAH-NAH-NAH-NAH
Didn't realize the girls were wise to his spi-el.
NAH-NAH-NAH-NAH-NAH
NAH-NAH-NAH-NAH-NAH
Huff-and-puff as though he had the ultimate ze-al

And always showing off like the Emperor Ne-ro.
Big bad Awmie thought he had the big ap-pe-al.
NAH-NAH-NAH-NAH-NAH (You poor dear,)
NAH-NAH-NAH-NAH-NAH (You need a big hug!)

Stuck-up Awmie thinks his tongue is all that mat-ters.
NAH-NAH-NAH-NAH-NAH
NAH-NAH-NAH-NAH-NAH
The fact that others matter too has left him shat-tered.
NAH-NAH-NAH-NAH-NAH
NAH-NAH-NAH-NAH-NAH
Now he works himself into a pet-u-lant lat-her
And steaming up his ears like the Emperor Ne-ro.
Stuck-up Awmie thinks his tongue is all that mat-ters.
NAH-NAH-NAH-NAH-NAH (Naughty boy,)
NAH-NAH-NAH-NAH-NAH (You *must* learn discipline!)

Little Aw-mie thinks that he's a great big he-ro.
NAH-NAH-NAH-NAH-NAH
NAH-NAH-NAH-NAH-NAH
Poor boy didn't know that he's really a big ze-ro.
NAH-NAH-NAH-NAH-NAH
NAH-NAH-NAH-NAH-NAH
Shoulda known he should've tried for some great deal-o
Instead of blowing off like the Emperor Ne-ro.
Little Aw-mie thinks that he's a great big he-ro.
NAH-NAH-NAH-NAH-NAH
NAH-NAH-NAH-NAH-NAH

Little Awmie thinks that he's
A great big hero
A great big hero
A great big hero
Little Aw-mie thinks that he's a great big he-ro.
NAH-NAH-NAH-NAH-NAH!
NAH-NAH-NAH-NAH-NAH!

Now when Awmie heard that one he was so excited be went beside himself and caused such a scene (a scene so harrowing in its unleashing its depiction will have to wait for another time) that he really had to be restrained, and so we leave our story with the aftermath of that rather long ordeal, in which Professor Doodlemax offers some parting consolation words to the oversized lad: "Now-now-now son, I'm afraid you're just-just-just going to have to realize...that-that-that things are just not-not-not like the old days....we-we-we are no longer the only important ones in existence...yes-yes-yes it hurt me to realize that too-too-too...but-but-but others are just so-so-so-insistent...that they-they-they too are important, and worst-worst-worst of all...just as important...as-as-as ourselves...we've tried, son...we-we-we've tried...but I fear-fear-fear...we'll just have to learn to adjust...some facts...some...facts...are like that...they happen...they just happen..."

Thy Love Vamp

"*Ayyyy Professor!*" Vamp cried with ridicule as she tightened her neck-hold for a brief moment. "You're supposed to giddiyap and not only aren't you doing so, you seem to want to wiggle away from me! But *oo-oo-ooh* am I enjoying this mount *ha-ha-ha-hahhh!*"

Paloma could only grunt in a mixture of rage, frustration and a touch of humiliation. Vamp's voice, cackling straight into her ear, seemed to resonate all the more, in accompaniment with the roar of the patrons and the popping of flashes; Vamp's heavy breathing threatened to mold her straining, pulling body. The neck-hold around her throat made it difficult for her to breathe; one arm and hand flailed at the air, futilely grasping for something---and what was the mini-battle below---dueling stilettos? Vamp's foot was pushing against hers---she was trying to push Paloma's shoe off (and only Paloma's determination prevented Vamp from succeeding)! Vamp, who had the rest of her entrapped, was clearly teasing her in this manner as well ("oh you're so close to losing it Professor"); actually Vamp had nearly lost *her* own shoe a few times in the attempt, an irony Paloma would have found amusing were she not otherwise helpless underneath this heifer(!), that, coupled with the other patrons sitting or standing and watching with fascination and the cameras, still and motion, devouring all this, made Paloma's fury all the more intense---why didn't anyone intervene or try to help her? Surely they could see she was in need of help! *Help me blast you HELP ME!* she wanted to scream. *Don't you realize what's happening?* That should surely be obvious!

And Horace? Isn't that Horace who just came in? It *was--is! WHY DOESN'T HE DO SOMETHING?*

"Why Professor!" Vamp shrieked delightfully, "look who's here! Your man---soon to be ex-man, that is---is in the house! What a prize…he's come to watch me kick your *edgie-kay-ted* derriere *heehee!*"

This sent Paloma squirming in desperation, squealing incoherently, nails scrawling, foot flexing and toes groping for both traction and to keep her blasted shoe on despite Vamp's efforts to separate them.

"Oh that woke you up did it!" Vamp teased. "But it's no use honey, your Horace is good as mine."

Paloma felt her body go limp yet again with exhaustion underneath Vamp's well-toned musculature. She sank her face down to the well-worn finish of the floor, eyes clenched shut, not even bothering to resist the water forming within them. All her mind could do was wander to happier times…

It had been almost twenty years since the marriage of Paloma Wilde and Horace Percival, sweethearts who had met during their freshman year in college. By this time Paloma had long since been groomed into moving beyond the childishness of wanderlust and inquiry and rambunctiousness to such a degree that she now had only vague memories of ever having been remotely interested in such things; she had become what was referred to her as "a *proper* lady!" Psychology had been her major, with Library Science as a minor, and she had excelled at both beyond all expectations, graduating with honors and earning her doctorate by her late twenties, becoming Dr. Paloma Percival, respected professor of Psychology at a major university and author of such books as *The Hidden Unexplored Beast Within the Most Refined Human* and with publications of selected essays as *Examinations and Observations of Dr. Paloma Percival*. Horace, though a nice enough man (and certainly one who would never have hurt his wife in the least way) by the standards Paloma had had groomed into her, seemed to a degree to be a bit below them; the enforcers would have preferred that he had had the dominant share of occupation and income. He had met Paloma in a Psychology class they had both been taking, but he was a Social Work major who had unexpectedly switched to Photography, which he eventually graduated in. Unlike his wife, he had elected to stop his studies at the Masters Degree, after which he began what would be an equally respected career as a photographer with numerous exhibits of his work to his credit. Still, any observer could conclude that the Percivals had been very much made for each other.

There were no children. At first some of the more narrow-minded skeptics (and relations) presumed that this was a key factor in what would become their current predicament, but those who knew, understood and accepted the Percivals were better positioned to discount such speculation. They were ideal, loving and well-loved together and individually (though Paloma, often seen in the attire [if not the temperament] of a "Sunday school matron," seemed a tad repressed to those with acute sensitivity), each was quite successful in their chosen line of work.

But then came Vanessa "the Vamp" Johnson.

Paloma had recognized her from photo spreads in several magazines. Founder and Chief Executive Officer of Vamp Enterprises, named for the nickname earned her by her reputation (and rumored approach) for moving in on a person or company or whatever and taking it for her own. Paloma then remembered that Horace had recently done a couple of photo spreads for her. Looking at the photo spread, she had had to admit the Vamp *was* quite stunning---tall, shapely as only one who worked out fanatically could be, flawless milk-chocolate skin, early thirtyish, and virtually any attire she wore seemed made *for* her---usually (in the photo spreads) these were stylish conservative business attire, but with a touch of dare in places, a deceptively wicked smile, classic pumps with the heel maybe too high or too thin; a little bit of cleavage (either bust of toe) showing---she made quite an impression even for those not at all interested in her.

But something had warned Paloma that her interest in Horace was not solely of a business one. That had been a letter to him from Vamp Johnson for yet another shoot.

"Uh…Horace…this Vamp Johnson wants *another* session with you…"

"Yes, but I told her she may have to wait a while. My calendar's packed for the next couple of weeks. Quite a number of major clients this time of year."

"Still, most of them don't usually ask for three sessions in almost as many weeks."

"Yes, that *is* unusual. But then Ms. Johnson is a most unusual person."

"No kidding."

"What's *no* kidding, dear Paloma, is my love with *you*." And he had hugged and kissed her. It had seemed genuine enough. *Still…*

One morning the following week, a perplexed Horace found himself adjusting his calendar.

"Now that's something!" he had said incredulously to Paloma. "Several of my clients cancelled on me unexpectedly…and along with that, a reminder from Vamp Johnson."

"About that third session."

"Yeah…I guess I do have room for her now."

"Horace…please be careful," she had said, suspecting something.

"Relax, honey. It's just one last session."

Paloma could not bring herself to relax, especially given the Vamp's reputation for getting what she wanted. What if she now wanted Horace or his business? Those clients who had cancelled on him so unexpectedly had been longtime clients of his...what had happened? Had they been bought off or threatened by her? She hadn't really believed there was any affair going on, but if her suspicions about Vamp were true, what Horace---or Paloma---wished might not matter at all.

A few days later Paloma was in her office at the university, going over some of her students' class papers, checking over them and going over them repeatedly, making sure she was interpreting them correctly and assigning the proper grade ("like a *proper* lady!"). She had just completed them when she jolted with a start at the sight of a statuesque businesswoman who had entered without her notice.

"Very meticulous of you, Professor," the Vamp smiled. "It's no wonder you're so respected in the highest of places."

"Well...what brings you here?"

"There's no need to feign coyness. The truth is---I *do* want Horace Percival. The business..." Her smile widened. "...and the man."

"How *considerate* of you to tell me that," Paloma had replied icily.

"Considerate..." Vamp mused. "That's not an adjective many would describe me as, especially not after I've acquired their items or companies away from them. You see, Professor, that's the way things are today. Take or be taken. Some are the hammer, others are the anvil to be pounded on. Survival of the fittest."

"Of which *you* are most fit."

"Aw don't take it so hard, Professor. Times do change you know. Your way worked well for you and Horace...*then*. But things changed...where I come from, you've got to take what you want...kill or be killed...not *literally*, mind you. But you see, you're an old hat intellectual dilettante...and we need *action*, not words; passion, not ration. I can give Horace plush assignments, prestige, status, social position..." She abruptly stared down at Paloma. "...maybe even some *children*."

"And what makes you think Horace wants *anything* from you?"

"Oh, he is a tough nut to crack; you've tied his rein real tight all right. But he'll find me a preferable new model, he just doesn't realize it. Prepare yourself for the pasture, Professor...*by-e-e-e...*" She glided outside with a ballerina's rush before Paloma could open her mouth to order her out.

"That's so crazy!" Horace had exclaimed when Paloma had informed him of the exchange. "I just don't understand her obsession...but that settles it, Paloma. No more sessions with Vamp Johnson."

"It...it just makes me so sick to have that---that predator after you---after both of us," Paloma replied, still shaken. "Luckily I'd completed the grading just as she arrived or I'd never have been able to do so."

"Don't worry, honey," he reassured her, "she comes around the studio again, I'll tell her no, and never to address you in that way again! I mean that."

And he had, as Vamp learned when she called his studio. Surprisingly, she had taken that maturely enough, as he reported to Paloma, and for the next couple of weeks, there had been no sign of Vamp Johnson in the sights of either of the Percivals. Apparently that had been that.

Or so Paloma (and Horace) had thought.

One evening she had finished doing herself in the best "Sunday church matron" attire; she was to meet Horace at a reception later that evening. She had been looking forward to it, for it was honoring an old mutual now-retired teacher of theirs from their undergraduate years that both loved and respected.

Not even the fading memory of Vamp Johnson could dampen her mood.

The ring of her telephone put a stop to her looking at herself in the mirror.

"Hello, Percival residence."

"Is this Mrs.---er, Dr. Percival?"

"Speaking."

"Oh thank goodness! You must come at once---something's happened to your husband."

"*Horace...?*" she gasped in fright. "What is it---what---"

"I---I really can't discuss it over the phone. You need to hurry---*hurry!*"

"O---okay okay---give me the address."

Writing it down, she listened to the directions, then assured the caller that she would be over and rushed out.

She had found it rather odd at the address, and yet everything was accurate; this was where she had been told to go. "The Pachyderm Tavern? A *bar club?* But Horace doesn't drink...why would he have ventured here? Unless...he ran into someone he knew there and remained long enough for---" But this was no time for speculation, Horace needed her help.

"Horace...*Horace!*" she cried as she rushed inside. It was a simple enough tavern, but the arrangement seemed unusual, for all the chairs and tables were backed in the corners, the bar was also backed against a wall, a police alarm was near by, and there were two television cameras, a few patrons...but not Horace.

"Where...where is he? Where's my husband? I was told he needed me here---"

Silence.

"Is this a practical joke or---"

"*SURPRISE!!!*" roared a too-familiar voice.

She whirled her head just in time to see Vamp spring and pounce upon her as a lioness would a prey.

"Wake up, Professor!" Vamp's squeal snapped Paloma back to reality. "I'm getting tired and you're daydreaming instead of conceding!"

Paloma kept her reply to herself. "Well, that was quite easy of that Vamp to subdue me like this...tricking me into coming to this tavern...like a fly flying right into the spider's web." She looked all around her, at the hubbubing patrons, the bartender, all the cameras, Horace...and even what little of the Vamp she could view. No more tears or whimpering---she had to concentrate on her predicament and just how she could find a way out of this and hopefully keep her dignity...think...think...

Her mind came to something...a potential...something from early in her childhood, something that had been nearly forgotten behind all the grooming, all the admonitions about being "a proper lady." That childhood adventurer...the long-suppressed tomboy...the one who could hold her own even against some bigger boys. The "proper lady" had had no preparation for this particular contingency...but just maybe the now-summoned wanderluster could. All she needed was some sort of opening...

"Professor, oh Professor," Vamp murmured. "Say something heehee---" She moved her face close to Paloma's, loosening her hold slightly and involuntarily.

That was when Paloma did something. She thrusted her head with one swift movement, ramming it into Vamp's face. Vamp gave a throaty cry and threw her hands onto her face. Paloma seized the moment and pushed-threw herself away from Vamp, scrambling as far as she could before rocketing herself to her feet. A bit out of practice, maybe, but it was effective. The patrons, the bartender, and Horace stood frozen in disbelief.

Even more so was Vamp. Coming to her senses, she staggered to her feet and ran one hand over her face, then recoiled at the mild trickle of blood that had come from her nose. She snapped her head towards the still heavily-breathing Paloma.

"A nice trick for an old hat, Professor," she said with undisputable menace. "But I'll make you suffer all the more." She began to charge at Paloma, who somehow felt a sense of bravery as she kicked her shoes off (of *her own* free will!), then, as the Vamp had almost reached her, threw herself forward, impacting with her attacker's midsection at surprising speed. Paloma braked herself right after; Vamp fell back and sat down quite hard. Paloma stepped back, saturated neither by bravado or self-effacement. It was as though this part of her nature had never been lost.

With a roaring fury Vamp shot upright, jerking her belt of her waist and, charged at Paloma, ready to lash her with it. But Paloma was ready; she caught the belt in mid-air and yanked it, pulling Vamp towards her.

"Really, Ms. Johnson," she found herself saying as she grasped Vamp with a headlock, "I'm not supposed to get that until *after* I've done this." She pressed a certain spot in Vamp's neck and Vamp's face went blank just before her body went limp. "Oh dear, I forgot to ask how you like your own medicine...the necklock, that is." She turned to the awe-struck bartender. "Here, take care of her," she told him, giving him Vamp's limp form, as she turned to the equally awed Horace.

"I...learned from the neighbor you'd come to this address," he said shakily, anticipating her queries. "I'm...so sorry I wasn't..."

"Don't apologize...or explain," she said reassuringly. "In a sense, I think I needed this." She turned to one of the cameramen. "What's with the cameras and stuff?"

"We were hired by Ms. Johnson to shoot this pilot for a reality show, Dr. Percival," the cameraman replied. "To show off her various adventures and personal projects."

"Starting with trying to acquire my husband and humiliating me," she said provocatively.

"Well...yes."

"Really," she mused, more intrigued than anyone would have dared to expect. "So what is the name of this show?"

"*Thy Love Vamp.*"

"This whole thing was orchestrated by Ms. Johnson," the bartender added.

"I see," Paloma replied, then looked at Vamp, who, still unconscious, had been laid out on the bar. "Well, when the Vamp comes to, tell her thanks."

"*Thanks...?*"

"For enabling me to find myself once more." She turned back to the cameraman. "Are your cameras still rolling?"

"Yes."

"Well, here's a possible finale for the show *Thy Love Vamp.*" She moved to retrieve her shoes. She bent over as if about to put them back on but paused, then elected to simply carry them as she continued, determined, to Horace. Patting his shoulder with energy, she said to him in a tone that was matter-of-fact yet was beaming and had a hint of a dare to it: "Let's go!"

"Yes...yes...*yes,*" Horace remarked, and the Percivals, arm in arm, stepped out of the Pachyderm Tavern, in which a concession of light applause followed. Vanessa "the Vamp" Johnson would simply have to catch it on the broadcast.

Sisters Yabarre!

"Frances Yabarre,
Frances Yabarre,
Rise up to the stars,
O Frances Yabarre.
Frances Yabarre,
Frances Yabarre,
She sends us so far.
She's Frances Yabarre!"

So went the anthem, by now legendary around these parts, celebrating yet another honor for the one and only Frances Yabarre. By now it no longer mattered what the nature of the honor was, only that Frances Yabarre had secured another honor to add to her infinite collection of awards, honors, and citations.

Kaolind, used to it all by now, observed nonplussed at the spectacle. For her this was even more of an eternity than it would have been for another, for she had observed her sister Frances achieve all kinds of honors from their childhood on--- the beauty pageants, top of her classes, a many-time valedictorian, trophies, and several local radio and TV shows, a few of which had extended into higher ranges. A part of Kaolind was immensely proud of her sister, and another part, she had had to admit, was quite resentful since her own accomplishments (and there *were* quite a few of her own!) seemed overshadowed, or at least not mentioned in ways that featured as prominently in the scene as Frances'---indeed, Kaolind was considered by many as a ne'er-do-well, which rankled her to no end.

Given her druthers, Kaolind would not have bothered to be here at all, for such events, despite her pride in Frances, tended to bring out the mood in her, and rarely more so than this time, for this particular honor, Frances had prevailed astoundingly over a runner-up who had literally "thumped"

Kaolind herself from the competition. This after local voices had fantasized loudly of a Yabarre versus Yabarre competition, which Kaolind's defeat had silenced. (Ironically lost in all the hubbub was the fact that the one time that sisterly round had occurred, it had been *Kaolind* who prevailed; of course that was an ancient fluke [or so the voices droned]). Again, had she had her druthers, Kaolind would never had shown up here. But protocolic pressure prevailed ("for the sake of family unity!" many had bleated), and so she found herself a part of the attendance roster.

The lights became as dim as Kaolind's mood and a tuxedoed emcee stepped out to start speaking.

"And now," Kaolind droned in silent unison with his exalted cry, "I wish to commence this event honoring our most beloved of favorite daughters---one of our local queens! Our ever-lasting star of the show---*MISS FRANCES YABARRE!*" And the roaring applause greeted Frances as she stepped out, beaming, onto the podium. Most in the room stood up in a wild ovation. Kaolind did not stand up.

"Now, Frances," the emcee went on, "I would like to present you, on behalf of our mayor, the key to the city, and this certificate of honor, whereas..." Kaolind made no effort to hear the words clearly or get them down; she'd heard it all before. "...I hereby declare this to be *FRANCES YABARRE DAY!*" More applause, more ovation, as the emcee proudly awarded the certificate to Frances, whose disbelieving smile of acceptance brought on what Kaolind could only refer to in silence as "still more ovation."

"Ladies and gentlemen," Frances said with quiet humility, "I...I can't begin to say just how much this honor means to me. All I can say is that...I shall do my best to prove myself worthy of that which you have bestowed upon me..." ("*As you always do, dear sister,*" Kaolind muttered to herself)

"…for, to be quite blunt, I would not be worth so much trouble without you and your support---from the greatest people on this earth!" She waved, curtsied, then stepped off the podium with the pedigreed elegance of one with lengthy experience of such moments.

"*Frances Yabarre!*" cried the emcee. "Let's hear it once more for Frances Yabarre!" And the crowd burst into the "Frances Yabarre" anthem again. Kaolind remained nonplussed.

Kaolind efforted a poker face throughout all the conversation about Frances as she gathered up items from the elaborate buffet. Her brow lowered in a fuming glare as she noted among them the Reverend St. John Clipper, known quite well for haranguing her in sermons and print about her repeated "spurns" of one Donald Ignatz, the "MAN'S man" she needed to "whip" or "beat" her into shape as though she were some cross between clay and an egg. The crowds were sufficiently packed she could not easily get away, but she tried to keep herself as inconspicuous as possible so as to avoid another lecture. However the queries, at her or not, persisted.

"So, what do you say about your sister?"

"After all, *she* was the one the runner-up beat for the honor."

"Well…" (Frances.) "…you know we try not to…discuss that."

"But you *know*, of course, of the petition campaign to rename the Kaolind Yabarre *Forum*…to the Frances Yabarre Gold Room…"

"Frances Yabarre Gold Room…how romantic!"

"Yes…*Forum* is just so…formal."

"How true…you hear anything of this rumor they're planning to shift the name of Kaolind Yabarre Arena after that of that cousin of theirs…Josephine I believe her name is?"

"Oh, I don't know for sure…but it does seem poor Kaolind's losing all her honors, does it not?"

"Well, like I said---" (Reverend Clipper.) "---it would have been much better for her if she'd accepted the offer of that nice honorable Mr. Donald Ignatz---but she re-JECTED him not once but TWICE! Now if that had been our great queen Frances there---"

"More's the pity for Frances…but then we all have our bad lumber in our woodpiles."

"True, true…what's so special about Kaolind anyway?"

That was the last straw for Kaolind. And practically in her ear! Within seconds she had whirled around and slammed her tray onto the table of the ones who had said the last two remarks, the violent crash startling not only that table's guests but everyone else.

"That's just enough!" she exploded. *"It is Frances this, Frances that! Pay NO attention or respect to third rate Kaolind---she's just a miserable ne'er-do-well! Bad lumber! Nobody special!"* The guests, shocked out of their euphoria, stood mute, as if only realizing what they had just unleashed.

It was Frances, equally startled by Kaolind's outburst, who was first, after a time, to speak. "Now…Kaolind…" she said as delicately as possible, "…you know that's not really true…"

But that only caused Kaolind to turn on her. *"Do I, Frances? DO I REALLY?"* she snapped before turning back to the crowd as a whole. "Kind of hard to TELL when every other syllable that isn't about my GOD-honored sister is a none too thinly-veiled jibe at me, as if I was not quite as good---or worthy of any honors---as her or even *my cousin Josephine---AGAIN!"*

She turned back on Frances. "And you said *NOT ONE WORD* to defuse that---or bother to donate one micro-iota of the love and praise and honor showered on you to even offer a minor shout-out to your own sister's effort, as short as it fell now and usual."

Frances felt her heart sank, realizing that all Kaolind had said was true. She had been so caught up in the accolades given her for her accomplishments that she had neglected to think of her sister's disappointment at not making the final round, as well as other recent developments.

"And not only *that*," Kaolind continued, "some of you even have the gall to denude what *few* accomplishments I *have* achieved---that proposal to change the Kaolind Yabarre Forum to the *Frances Yabarre Gold Room!* And the Kaolind Yabarre Arena to the Josephine Yabarre Arena too! AND---" She glared at Reverend Clipper. "---who are YOU---or *ANY* of you---to lecture me on who I go with in my life! WHO, WHO *WHO?*" She sank to the floor, her fury spent. "If only that was all! But why should I expect anything more...nobody loves Kaolind Yabarre...nobody loves me..." With a fading wail, she sank to a near-fetal position, sobbing uncontrollably, as all looked on in degrees of sympathy and horror. Frances, looking at her in anguish, stood at a loss over what to say or do, and fighting the urge to weep herself. If only she had paid attention---how the comparisons others had made between her and Kaolind, clearly in her favor, had affected her sister, who had always been considered second-best at most. She stood frozen over her own culpability in this, as a few people gently approached Kaolind and eased her to her feet, murmuring reassuring words to her as they helped to guide her to another end of the room. Frances could only look on sadly at the scene.

"*WOOOO!*"

The high-pitched sound startled Frances out of her stupor. She turned to it and immediately recognized its source. That hotshot up-and-comer Cain Harvard, already fiddling with his camera phone. Frances realized in horror that he had likely filmed everything that had just occurred.

"Yeah---!" he beamed at nobody in particular. "Mmmmm *boy* are they really gonna eat this up!" He began to rush towards the nearest exit, which meant he would bypass Frances. His tone indicated to her that he had not yet sent the word. Frances noted his obliviousness to all, including her. She had only instants to act. At the right moment she jutted her foot forward, in time for Harvard's foot to collide with hers. Harvard's camera phone sailed through the air, its owner instinctively stretched and flailed his arms in a futile attempt to avoid impacting with the floor. Seconds after Harvard's landing, his camera phone struck a pillar sharply, shattering into pieces.

Frances gasped in feigned shock. *"Oh---!* I---I'm so---so sorry...I didn't...didn't mean...!"

But Harvard's focus was on his shattered camera phone. "My scoop!" he gasped, frantically regaining his equilibrium too late. *"L---lost!"* he cried, choking three sobs at this realization.

As the crowd rushed to console Harvard, Frances, aware of her limited window of opportunity, dug with urgency through her pockets. *Oh, I hope I---YES! There it is!* She pulled out a camera phone of her own, and, aware that this could well be the most important message---and definitely the most urgent one---she might ever send, used it to type out a message of her own, praying and hoping as she'd rarely done at other times.

The following day, the news had surprisingly little to say about the latest awards ceremony honoring Frances Yabarre; instead, readers on online and print were treated to a special report focusing on the accomplishments and charity of Kaolind Yabarre.

And so the cycle continues…

Marybel After the Genocide

He watched from behind as she ascended the stairs with a determination about her this once upon a time. Each well-placed step she took, whether firmly placed on a step or flexibly lifting it off, somehow accentuated the fitness of her slender sixty-seven inch body. Even in this state he could still admire a woman's body, its movement and its muscularity. Well at least he had not lost *all* of the abilities of his corporeal self. He continued to watch over her as she pushed herself upward to the top of the stairs.

"Well, Marybel, you're home at last," she said to herself upon reaching that goal, in an ironic attempt at humor. "Another day gone and I'm home at last." She paused. "Or as close to home as I'm likely to get for a good long while." She opened the door to her room. "Such is the life for I, Marybel Sultan, reduced to a lifetime as boarder and caretaker to a hapless veteran of the same thing that reduced me to this. Funny thing is it wasn't war wounds that landed him in his predicament." She entered the doorway but paused a yard inside her room; he followed closely from behind.

"Barely two years since the Genocide," she went on with a sigh, "and less than that since my attempt to go out…to fulfill what the will of the people have craved for---*humph*---a year since I arrived here."

Then she suddenly turned around.

"You know," she blazed in an indignant snap, "it's not *that* nice to watch so closely. Yes my friend, I'm wise to you, and spare me the inquiry of how too."

He was stunned. That should not have happened. But then neither should just about everything else about his current state.

In shock, embarrassment and a bit of humility he rushed away, as if catapulted by Marybel's outburst, and glided over and along the stairway, through the halls and the walls, until he came to the makeshift room where the prostrate form, lying on its back was a peaceful though catatonic sleep.

If only.

It had occurred barely a month after he had returned to civilian life after amassing several commendations and medals for outstanding service to one's country. Service indeed---murder for the pettiest of reasons. But he had obeyed---just like a good soldier.

The good soldier who would soon after be rear-ended in his car on the way home from an errand for his mother. The good soldier who, after stopping the ethnic-slurring, rowdy-ridden car, had confronted them about their behavior---and got a meeting with shotgun ammunition for his efforts. How quick that thing could be cocked.

He had next felt himself floating in some unknown sort of void, seeing visions of various activities down below, most notably and shockingly the sullen conversations between his mother and hospital doctors concerning the fate as a potential vegetable of the comatose man on life support in the hospital bed---himself. The head---*his* head---was heavily wrapped in bandages already getting splotched with red. The initial shock of that sight caused him to float away from there, through the ceiling and several floors, into the air far above the ground.

It had taken him a little bit of time to get an idea of his state, and the theme of the Africans flying back to Africa in the folk tales came to mind. It had been a most tempting idea for him, but somehow something told him that there was a different reason for his being in this form. It was a matter of finding out what the purpose was? (And could he still do the wheets and the whews?)

In the meantime, he had learned over the time since that he could travel in and out of his physical form, and could travel and fly at near-instantaneous speeds (in other words, as far or as fast as his mind could imagine), and, under certain circumstances, track persons down by tracing their mental imprints. (And it was good for close-ups of the *femmes*, he quickly learned.)

He had discovered another skill in pursuit of the rowdies who had shot him. Though not given to frivolous pursuits, he had had to allow himself this sweet justice. After he had tracked them to a certain bar (of course!), he had noticed laughing, drinking and having a good time. Incensed, he had charged at them---and right through them. But as he did, he noticed they had had a degree of disorientation, then shakily left the bar, to the surprise of many. Good. Served them right if they had been rendered sick.

The following morning he had realized what he had done when he saw the newspaper story in which it was revealed that the rowdies had all turned themselves in---and all without a single lead!

"Lord, it's so unbelievable...!" his mother had beamed as she had shown the newspaper to him. "I know you can't whoop and holler with me but look! Those boys who shot you went and surrendered. Ain't that a real godsend!" Though he could not physically respond, it had warmed him to see her in a buoyant mood again, even if only until the euphoria waned and the reality of a catatonic son set in once more. Still, he had become aware of what he could do---and of the responsibility it carried.

It had been shortly after that that a boarder had come to stay with them and to assist in his care. Though the greetings had been pleasant, and the warm smile that had greeted him was genuine, he could sense a vivid melancholia within her, and an air of mystery behind her. Not that she had been engaged in deception---he would have spotted that with considerable ease--

-but there was something within that had given him an ominous feeling.

The moniker, Marybel Sultan, had sounded familiar to him---this fashion model---that was it! She had been a fairly prominent model who was said to be on her way to hitting the big time. Then she had disappeared from the pages suddenly--- at *roughly the same time as the Genocide*. Now he had gotten the message, as far as Marybel's history was concerned.

Yet this was not the whole of his mission of sorts. That, whatever it was, was still to be deduced. (Still, someone to wheet and whew---however silently.)

The click of the front door snapped him out of his memories and sent him rushing towards it even though he knew that it was his mother returning from her nurse's aide job. He followed her through the rooms and halls until she came to his room where his body laid in serene sleep.

"Oh---you're already asleep," she murmured. "Well, ain't no sense in disturbing you...you're obviously at peace for tonight."

Would that he really were. But he followed her upstairs as she trudged up into the hallway, where she knocked on Marybel's door.

"Yes...?" Marybel's voice inquired.

"It's me, honey. I just wanted to make sure all was well."

"It is...did he wake up?"

"No, he's still asleep. You sure know how to care, Marybel. Good night, now, have you your own good sleep."

"You too. 'Night."

He observed her as she let herself in her own room. Perceiving that she was now safe and sound, he turned his thoughts back to Marybel. Now he knew for sure that, though his shock and embarrassment had prevented him from realizing it earlier, she was the reason for his mission. She was aware of his presence and had spoken directly to him; not even his mother had proven able to do that. He still did not fully understand this, but he expected that he would learn all when the time and need were right. How dense he could be, he fumed---it had been a big part of why he was now in his predicament. But now he had to play out the hand, as though he were in a bizarre real-life version of the card games he loved to play when he and his body had been one in the same. He glided through Marybel's door.

Her room was a shrine of sorts to the now-destroyed career she had devoted so much energy building. The glossies, photos, advertisements for various cosmetics, the posters and covers, all of which were of her face, the body waist up, the body in casual wear, evening attire, swimsuits, pants, dresses, blouses, sweatshirts et cetera---some bearing the name *Marybel Sultan*, others simply saying *Marybel*, and still others with no name at all, for most had been made for those who had already known who she was, and those who did not would have learned that before long. And that did not include the commercials or TV appearances which she would constantly play over and over on a VCR as if they were all she had left of her existence (which in a sense they were). There were a few unopened crates of the perfume *Marybel* in a corner of her closet. And if his memory was serving him correctly, there had even been talk of a movie deal.

"Such was the career of Marybel Sultan," she would often sigh when alone in her room. "Or Marybel. Or...me." Then she sang a small part of a Stevie Wonder song: *"Too high...too high...but I ain't touched the sky...,"* wondering if she meant her career or herself---the ultimate crime of being born an Iraqi-American. She would still be *Marybel*, the name over photos and layouts in magazines and the perfume that had barely been out two days before that damned Genocide which had destroyed a large part of her family, particularly that shelter whose name could be presumed by some xenophobe as a corruption of the name America. Her portfolio contained a bunch of clippings about that disaster. Her family had not approved of her venturing out into the world of modeling, and especially not by eschewing marriage and domesticity for that career, now as much a casualty of the Genocide as the innocents made controversial and dangerous for who they were rather for anything they had done other than having the misfortune of the wrong "leader" who hindered some black drops from superpowered machinations. No one---not family, agents, colleagues, or fans-turned-enemies---had wanted any more to do with her, some had wanted to see her dead. Family considered her dead, the cause of the loss of loved ones.

Finally, defeated by everyone and patriotism, she had tried to fulfill their wishes. *"Your wish is my command,"* she had mocked when she took the razor to her wrists. Too bad she had neglected to close her hotel room more securely, otherwise a pageboy would not have caught the gaze of her unconscious form and the small puddles of blood underneath her wrists and rushed to her aid while summoning help. So much for satisfying the masses.

Now there she was, after several months in a sanitarium, two more in transition, and a semester in the Work-Study program, now watching over a disabled veteran of the very same Genocide which destroyed her.

He understood the irony too well.

She knew he was there. "Oh---hi," she said. "Hey, I'm sorry about snapping at you earlier, but...well, I was tired and forlorn about what happened to me..."

86

She paused, and chuckled sarcastically. "What a fool I am, lamenting my own troubles to someone who had it even worse than me...you do seem to be making the best of it though."

If he had been able to speak he might have admitted that despite his discomfort and doubts, he was doing reasonably well, given his condition. He looked at her, seated in a partially Thinker position, head cupped in her hands, face still retaining its subtle melancholia.

"Funny," she continued wearily, "I'm here to help care for you, but methinks you're caring for me!" The irony sparked a quiet chuckle from her. "Listen---I'm terribly tired right now; I don't know about you in your...state, but *I'm* still in need of beauty sleep. Talk to you tomorrow during the walk, ok?"

He got the message. He reckoned sarcastically that perhaps being out of self may have spoiled him to some degree---he seemed to be forgetting that corporeal forms still needed rest and privacy.

Dropping through the floor, he made his way back to his room and into his body. That, at least, would need all the rest he could get if his mission was to succeed.

The walks with Marybel were his favorite part of the company she kept, and were virtually the only time in which he stayed within his physical body throughout. She was a gentle and patient guide, grasping his hand and assisting him as he made his halting steps and stared ahead of him perennially at the passersby and structures that would pass, and looking in other directions only at a sudden sound or when she spoke to him.

"You're making quite a progress," she would say with a sunny tone to him. "That's it...easy...yes, that's right." It pleased him to see her smile at him; he could tell that this took her mind off her own pain, which was another reason why this part of the day was so favorable to him. He nodded jerkily to show his appreciation (for he still could not speak even in physical form as yet), which usually caused her to blush a little.

He misstepped at a corner and would have fallen had she not wrapped her arms around his midsection. She was stronger than she appeared to be and was able to stop his fall. As she pulled him erect he shook and blinked wildly with frustration, more angry with himself than with her.

"Relax, relax," she said quickly with reassurance, trying to calm him down. "It's okay…there's no need to reproach yourself."

He made an effort, but it was hard. That bullheaded perfectionism was as formidable as ever.

"You'll get it right," she went on. "You've already advanced a lot."

He eventually did calm down, buoyed in large part by her presence and support. But a minor frustration remained--- this kind of humiliation would never have occurred outside this crippled form, in the air soaring smoothly above it all. But he stayed put, out of his dedication to Marybel. (And besides, he couldn't take her up there with him.)

"Well, helping the Samson stand upright I see!" barked a gruff, orderly and well-modulated voice that caused Marybel to turn in surprise. Sensing her start, he turned his head as best he could, to see a large graying man, dressed in a decorated military uniform, standing to attention and facing them with a decidedly paternal air. Something about this person bothered him, and it wasn't envy or jealously.

"Yes, this is indeed a mighty Samson," Marybel replied proudly, rendered indignant by the man's superior demeanor. "His body may be crippled but the mind remains strong despite the little bigots who crippled him after his service to his country in defense of those who would kill him and me."

"That so?" the man replied, jutting out his hand. "No need to be offended. Didn't know he also fought in service. Shouldn't have expected a cripple to join up in national crises anyhow. General Northman's the name."

Marybel shook Northman's hand with some begrudgement, but when the general turned to him, he feigned numbness in both hands. Northman took and shook his right hand, then backed away to speak again.

"Oh, he's that bad off, I see." Saluted. "Well, no point in arguing over spilled milk---or blood." Another salute. "Carry on...*soldier!*" And with that, plus a glance at Marybel, the general set off with extreme confidence. He could not tell if Marybel had actually seen the glance (though something in her seemed to light up at the moment), but *he* had, and he did not like the implications.

"Well, my friend," she said after a brief silence, "it's time for us to move on...we can both use the exercise."

She guided him forward; he cooperated with her for the rest of the walk, which was uneventful and pleasant, and found himself actually beginning to feel something for his guide. He shrugged it off, of course, for how could one consummate a relationship with one in his condition?

But he was certain of one thing: this Northman fellow merited himself a nice covert investigation.

It surprised him that he was feeing quite good about his ethereal self as he glided by the doings and drudgery of the city and its denizens. It was becoming (or more accurately, *had* become) second nature to him, though he retained a degree of difficulty accepting his state. Also, this is what he would have called a business trip, had he ever had a chance to work in the corporate world. He was on the trail of this General Northman, and had he been able to speak he might have cracked that the trail marking could be found by its noxiousity. But it did take a little while to follow it, and it led him much further away than he had anticipated.

The trail ended (at *last!*) at a small, unassuming apartment building a few short blocks from an abandoned military base. He realized that it had been the same base from which he had enlisted and had been trained in the arts of discipline and suppression, and which had since become a casualty of cutbacks not long after the Genocide. Another irony he could not verbally laugh at.

He could hear a voice barking marching orders from the upper-floor apartment, though these orders were nothing like those he had had to endure at the hands of killjoy drill instructors as a result of need and naiveté. He gingerly hovered towards the lit window and positioned himself to view whatever was going on inside.

"Hup-ta-da-BOOM! Hup-ta-da-BOOM!"

Curiosity aroused, he dropped himself inside the building where these orders were coming from. Jackpot---it was General Northman, marching in an almost-comical step formation as he threw darts with each *"BOOM!"* or *"DIE!"*

"Ma-ry-bel DIE! Ma-ry-bel DIE!"

And then he realized the picture was of Marybel's face on the dartboard, plus the jacket plopped disdainfully on an easy chair in a corner of the room---a jacket with lieutenant's bars. Before he could react fully to these sights, Northman spoke as if making a vow to some invisible rally of supporters.

"And so, dear Lord of Mercy and Vengeance, You have given me a sign this afternoon---the object of Your Humble Servant's goals to redeem the honor of this Great Country that has been deflowered and spoilt by the intrusion of Iraqi meat such as this womanly

creature---" He jutted an accusing finger at the picture of Marybel. *"---whom You have given me the privilege to find. And so it is that I shalt begin my search-and-destroy mission just as our own search-and-destroy mission has exterminated the rest of her befouled race, so shall---so MUST ---I subdue this last enemy of our Honored Land and redeem the dignity of our military which dared to expel me, Your Most Honored and Faithful Servant, from their midst and close down my base---the force of American GOOD! The target has been located---and the Hunt shall begin!*

"But first---" Northman declared, whirling down toward where he was in a manner that revealed knowledge that an observer was around, *"YOU, foolish and traitorous social counselor, shall be disposed of IMMEDIATELY!!!"*

Before he had a chance to react to Northman's finding him out, he was met with a blast of cataclysmic energy that catapulted him out of the building, through the skies all around him, and into the stratosphere, being sent and rended in virtually all directions at a velocity that could only be guessed at. He felt himself coming apart and consequently losing his very sense of individuality. So this was the end.

"For America---and her HonorrRRRRRRR!!!!" Northman's words were the last thing he heard.

Refused.

Marybel looked with resigned longing at the letter returned to her by the mail carrier while she had been walking her friend. Still unwilling to accept her back---that was still her family's answer. Would they never cease punishing her for that now-purged dream of stardom? Would she ever abandon her role as scapegoat for what had happened to the family members in the homeland? *She* wept for them too, especially when she had first learned of it. But alas (she sighed) somebody had to be blamed for the loss of a dozen family members, many of whom were quite revered, in one misdirected swoop. And the soldiers and institutions and armchair officials were *de facto* landlords of many of us---couldn't very well badmouth *them*, could we?

She used a razor to gingerly open the envelope after which she eased out the contents, pulled out the staple which had attached to the papers, and casually plopped them in a box for paper to be recycled. What did it matter if some nosy passerby read them? Maybe they could even someday be mementoes of the sad life of Marybel Sultan who dared to dream too high and fell as she was about to touch the sky---

The door clicked open.

"Marybel." His mother. "May I speak with you?"

This had startled her a little. "Why...why certainly. Is there...any trouble?"

"No, child," she replied gently, "at least not to do with you. I just wanted you to know up front that you've been doing very well with my boy. The doctors say he's making unusually fast progress. Whatever you've got for motivation, it seems to be working."

"I'm glad I've been able to contribute to that," Marybel replied. "I know this can't be easy for you."

"Or for you. I've seen those envelopes, I'm afraid."

"Oh..." Her voice dropped to a whisper.

"Just can't understand how any family can cast a child out---especially after that fool war. Seems like you're a casualty, too...but I guess I'm just prying..."

"It's all right..."

"Listen, Marybel. The doctors say he'll be just about ready to graduate before long, but you're welcome to stay as long as you wish. We owe you at least that much."

Marybel had to restrain herself from a distance. "Well, that's very kind of you---"

"Some of that, too, but it's also good humanity. And if

you give that humanity up, you've given away your victory to those who would destroy you. My boy sort of did that by enlisting and then being sent off to partake in the war, did real well too, and soon as he gets back gets near blown away by those lazy cracker boys. But at least they're all paying dearly for it now." She rose to her feet. "Whoa---said a little too much...but that's not what I wanted to say to you. Do what you will with the advice, Lord knows I'm not your mother---but I hope you'll pay it some mind anyway."

"Thank you very much," Marybel said with heartwarming appreciation, then, after the mother departed, she sat up to ponder what had been said to her.

But then she wondered---*where was the son?*

She was lost in thought as she strolled down the streets towards the business area. She had not expected the offer from his mother to stay indefinitely with them until such time as her family accepted her back in their fold and/or she was able to get back on her feet emotionally and financially. She was uncertain as to how to take that she was indeed wanted after all the troubles and traumas of the past year and a half.

And as if that was not enough, she was starting to develop a minor panic within her, for he had not returned to check up with her as they had arranged between them; worse still, he had not responded when she attempted to make mental contact with him. Had anything happened to him---or *could* it to one in his state? Should she have told his mother of this as insurance? She was flustered over what to do or think. Oh, it would have been so much easier had she succeeded in fulfilling the desires of the people...!

She thought she heard the thump of a snare drum at the outskirts of the business area. Turning, she thought she saw Northman in the distance waving with a mischievous grin to her to follow him. She moved in his direction, but he had disappeared. Or was he there? *He was there*, she mused in anger. She was in no mood for games; she stalked forward, her steps muscular and bold in defiance and determination. A mild hiss was caught by her ears. A snake's seduction---or the smoke departing her eardrums?

The snare again. She whirled with violence. Northman again, same grin, same wave. This time she eyed him ducking around a corner into what she knew was a blind alley. Her gait had a violence of its own---she would teach him! And yet, something told her to keep at it, to get everything done.

Upon entering the alley, she was surprised, at the fact that Northman was nowhere to be seen to be sure, but even more at the arrangement set up in it. Its walls were ringed by posts with the U.S. flag atop them, flanking at the dead end a clustered group of U.S. flags from various periods in history, above which was an enormous blow-up of a magazine cover featuring her visage, shot upwards on camera, as she stood in a mock-rendition of the Statue of Liberty, complete with torch, spiked hat and book. She remembered that shoot from about three years ago when she had been part of a cover story titled *The New American Model: Of All Shapes, Sizes and Colors*. But scratched digitally in letters of red were the words *BLASPHEMER DIE!*

Just as this began to sink the snare thumped abruptly, as though right in her ear. She spun about to see Northman giving her a very cold stare.

"*At last I have you, invader!*" he thundered. "The nerve you have got, you pretty little terrorist, to pass yourself off as American."

"I am an American!" she retorted defiantly.

"Still your blasphemous, alien tongue! By liberty and justice, you stand convicted by your race, religion and nationality. Staining our flag and red-blooded gumption by pretending to be one of us. We smashed your outpost and crushed your forces and loved ones, but we made the mistake of letting you live. But I shall rectify that mistake!"

"How dare you…!" Marybel hissed, ready to stand her ground.

"But we are not without heart," Northman continued as though not hearing her, "I shall not destroy you physically…humans do not crush slugs so blithely. Rather, I shall seed you so that your plague of a strain will bleed itself out with successive generations and you will be shamed to uselessness by your own people."

Marybel noted that a crowd had been slowly accumulating in curiosity at the entrance to the alley. Miserable little gawkers.

"And do not concern yourself with your mongrel friend," Northman added with cryptic severity. "I have already dealt upon him as fate such as one committing the worst type of treason deserves…I have completed what those young punks started."

"*NO!*" she shrieked in horror as much at this news as at the realization that her triumphantly smiling adversary had indeed known of their relationship.

"Did you really think I was unaware of who he was? His jungle culture is known for its strange and wondrous powers, but they are no match at all for supreme American ingenuity, and neither are your exotic black widow Theda Bara wiles. Your day of reckoning is here, Marybel Sultan, and you are *MINE!*"

Marybel stood in shock for a brief instant, at a loss over what to do as, her heart pounding like a timpani, she absorbed all that Northman had told her, attempting to remain as composed as possible. She reoriented herself just in time to dodge the ersatz general's lunge at her, and, summoning up her days as a high school sprinter, made a desperate spurt for escape.

However, the crowd of spectators burst into action as soon as she reached them, and several of them intercepted her, springing upon her almost at once and halting her flight.

"Let me go!" she screamed as she fought and kicked in a vain effort at resistance, but there were too many of them.

"*Never*, you terrorist!"

"You won't get away from us...we're real Americans!"

"We don't want your kind here!"

"Kill her! Kill her! *Kill-l-l-l her-r-r-r-R-R-R!!*"

"NO!" Northman shouted at them. "Let me have her--- she's no use to us dead."

Obediently, the mob relaxed their grip on Marybel, and somebody's kick in her buttocks catapulted her into Northman, who began to wage his own attack. Marybel struggled as ferociously as before in spirit, but was too physically exhausted by now to continue for long, and Northman forced her to the pavement, where she lay limp under him.

"Now little Marybel," he said with calm sternness as if to a subdued unruly child, "it's just you and us now. Your friend is no more and your inherent evil shall be purged."

She looked at the crowd in a silent last appeal for help. But they were murmuring "God Bless America" as though in the midst of a cathartic release. She noted that this was a quite diverse mix of ages, races, ethnicities, hair colors, complexions, languages and religions---a few might have been her own race, and the gender ratio seemed about equal.

At this sight, she went blank and emotionless. Perhaps this was to be her fate after all---to be a sacrificial lamb. Why try to fight anymore? Perhaps she would join her friend at least.

There now…there…

What is this…what…

Oh, are you beginning to stir now?

…was he being…shifted about…

Thank goodness…it's not anywhere near your time.

…like he was being…being…

Not with what you've still got to do.

…molded.

Snap out of it, my child.

…molded and rocked.

Of course! Didn't your mother ever rock you?

Well…he remembered that she had. (But not in what felt to be giant hands.)

Well, just consider me a mother of this land. Only on a slightly more celestial stage.

He wondered to himself what that had to do with anything until it hit him.

MARYBEL!

Wait…calm down. You were nearly blown apart. Lucky I've been watching this spectacle or you might be nonexistent now. It took quite some doing to collect your remains and put you back together.

He remembered everything now. Stupid, stupid, stupid! If he had some powers he should have known that possibly someone else might---

Keep calm, that's water under the bridge now. But use this, and the incident with those racist boys who put you in your state in the first place---not to be so impulsive in the future.

He realized this was sound advice. Was this---Mother Africa---who had saved him---

That's rich! You're only an ocean and a couple of continents off. Seriously, you're in my jurisdiction. But rest assured, she's as admiring of you as I. But seriously again---later for that. Marybel needs you!

He turned his face to his rescuer---and the sight stunned him.

Not exactly the type who gets the wheets and the whews, I'm afraid---but you might learn something from this too.   But go now...both your futures and your peoples depend on it!

He departed for the corporeal world at top speed.

Within instants he had reached the alley where the crowd was spectating Northman's subduing of Marybel. Noticing their acceptance of the ersatz general's actions, he fumed. How he wished he could kill them all in one fell swoop. But he had neither power or time to do that; the spirit who had saved him was right on two counts---he needed to learn a little self-control, and more important, saving Marybel had priority. But she looked so numb and defeated---was he already too late? No, he dared not think of that, he had to take action now.

At full speed he rocketed his way through the crowd and right into Northman. But---he ricocheted upwards, like a ball bouncing off the fanatic. Perplexed, he zoomed downwards to make another attempt to strike.

And again he bounced off Northman. Had he been solid he would have bowled into the crowd. And Northman barely seemed to notice other than a smirk aimed right at him.

He had to exert tremendous will power to avoid panic. No...no...remember what she said about overreacting...think, man, *think!* Only he could save Marybel---

And then it all became clear to him---he knew now what he had to do. If there ever was a time for that military battle training to hit home---enough.

With a silent prayer, he blasted forward one last time--- this time entering Marybel.

The resulting explosion of colors and lights informed him that he had guessed correctly. But he felt himself being pulled apart yet again---only this time he was coming together at the same time. He could not say how all this was possible, only that he was fading away from this plane of existence and that this time there was no apparent return. *Farewell, Marybel, it sure was nice to have known you.*

And yet he could not help but feel triumphant as all ceased about him.

Marybel's face opened wide as if shocked back to life. She let out a horrible yet liberating scream that might have been bottled up too long as it accumulated. The force was enough to cause Northman to hesitate for an instant---the same one in which the crowd stopped singing "God Bless America" in mid-verse, and the same in which Marybel realized the truth of what had just been done on her behalf, a realization that made her scream crack into an anguished wail, then near-blind rage.

Almost before she knew it her fist had impacted with Northman's face, sending him staggering backwards, and she had exerted an equally violent force in freeing herself of him and springing to her feet, invigorated with the essence that had been her friend.

"How could you!" she part-shrieked, part-roared as she delivered a hard kick to Northman, catching him before he could steady himself and sending him down clumsily on his buttocks. *"Do you know who---what I---have done!"* she growled in a voice that threatened to turn on anything in sight as she dared him to charge at her.

He attempted to do this, but she easily eluded him and then gave him an abrupt, insane shove into his cluster of flags, toppling them over like fragile tenpins. *"He was truly fulfilling what this---De-MOCK-Cra-Zee!---was supposedly founded on!!"* Marybel screamed at him, oblivious to the tears starting to stream down her face. *"---and you---"* She suddenly whirled to stare down the crowd, propelling her finger at it to implicate them. *"---and YOU---drove him to sacrifice himself for me because you were such a bunch of sheep that you were willing to see me sacrificed LIKE SOME HAPLESS LAMB! HOW---DARE---YOU!!!"*

The crowd mumbled with incoherent franticness within itself, reduced to stuttering disorientation at both this turn of events and at the force of Marybel's including them in her ire. Marybel paid no further attention to them than to a food wrapper just thrown away in some receptacle; she turned back to Northman, who struggled to regain his equilibrium as though not quite grasping how to do so.

"No...no..." he spluttered, *"...this cannot be...you were supposed to...supposed to..."*

"Supposed to WHAT?" she shouted. "Lie back and let you or your flocks take my dignity along with everything else? *HA!* I won't be undignified---or *unAmericanized*---by a pathetic un-American such as you."

"NOOOOOO!!!!" Northman cried as if he was about to die at being called un-American.

Just then, two policemen arrived onto the scene, pushing their way through the numbed crowd. Marybel, upon seeing them and expecting them to go for her, stood her ground, ready to fight to the death; she was angry and guilty and grief-stricken enough to wage war on anyone.

But to Marybel's surprise, the policemen snatched up Northman and grasped him between them and quickly handcuffed him. "Okay, soldier," one said to him, "time to call a truce and go to the peace zone."

"But I almost conquered my prey," Northman appealed. "I almost destroyed her."

"Looks to me like she almost conquered you...sir," the other officer quipped.

"What is---?" Marybel inquired.

"Oh this guy went daffy after that war mess---hadda be shipped out of the military and into the loony bin, only he escaped a couple of weeks ago---"

"Tell me son," Northman murmured, "am I an American? Am I?"

"The greatest American hero alive---*sir!*" the officer replied, then turned back to Marybel. "Not to worry though, ma'am---he's harmless as a fly."

"*Really,*" she replied gruffly, and turned away.

"Hey! Aren't you---" the other officer began.

But she had already started on her way, moving through the crowd as though it were a dump to be traversed quickly. Once she was in open air again, her days as a high school sprinter came to full focus and she made a frantic run, hoping she could still be of help to her friend's mother, even if he was gone.

She ran at a pace she thought herself incapable of attaining, and which made her think she could fly if she quickened herself any farther. She did not concern herself with stop signs or traffic signals; all that mattered was her destination. She had to be there, even if only to offer what little consolation she could to his mother who deserved better than this.

Her determination was such that she almost missed the house and then, after she had corrected herself and run up the path, she nearly impacted at full speed with the front door. She felt as if she were observing herself ringing the doorbell frantically. Though only a few seconds passed, it seemed like forever until the door opened.

"Good heavens, girl!" the mother said. "No need to ring so much. Come on---come on!" and before Marybel could reply, she was already being pulled by her arm swiftly through the rooms. "Some kind of strange happenings, I swear!"

"But why does she seem---*delighted?*" Marybel inquired to herself as soon as she could collect her thoughts enough to think. "This is a tragedy!"

The mother forced Marybel through the open door to her son's room, and it was there that Marybel gasped in shock and disbelief. For he was sitting up in the bed, mobility almost completely restored.

"*Ma-ry-bel,*" his voice whispered shakily.

Neither he nor Marybel were able to explain the exact workings of what had occurred (and of course neither of them ever revealed the story to anyone), but the effects remained with both of them. His doctors were beside themselves trying to determine how he had all of a sudden made a near-complete recovery. He would always retain a slight speech impediment and minor jerkiness in his movements due to the brain damage he had suffered, yet his intellect was as sharp as ever, and nothing stopped him from becoming one of the foremost writers and critical thinkers to set foot in all the places he visited (including the African ones he eventually did visit), keeping the pompous and ruthless on their toes as he propagated awareness and empowerment to those needing it most. To be sure, he missed his days as a spirit to a point, but he preferred the corporeal life---not much fun being unable to touch and hold (especially his eventual paramour Marybel Sultan), even if his wheets and whews were memories now. His mother didn't care *how* he came back, only that he *had*.

"General" Northman was transferred to a maximum-security mental hospital where he still remains to this day. No charge was ever filed against him for his assaults on Marybel Sultan, and every so often one must reportedly watch out for potential copycats or others who might try to force their wills on others---perhaps even Northman himself.

Although Marybel Sultan never returned to fashion modeling, she is in a way a model once more, as an activist who speaks out forcefully on various issues, and fighting to make certain that tragedies like the Genocide will never occur again. She never again attempted suicide, and had she not mentioned it herself, one would never have guessed that this ebullient, energetic speaker activist had ever been a suicidal nihilist. She and her savior-turned friend/life partner now reside in a converted warehouse in a neighborhood full of those they seek to empower and bring together and share a lifestyle free of authoritarianism, separatism, tradition, domesticity and marriage.

So what did you expect, a return to the way things were?

Author's Notes

The Ugly Salon is written in large part presenting the salon (among others) as a representation of Americana as America would like to see itself (Tripota being an anagram for patriot, for example), yet Hyman's experiences turn out to be, in a very real way, Americana as it is, particularly for the black male wanting to be a part of the group (the adage ending with "if you're black, get back" as an example).

The Story of Little Awmie--- Told in the style of a fairy tale, is all about the sufferings of one who's had it all his way for eternity, but now has to cope with the fact that the world is no longer solely *his* oyster---that he now has to "share the wealth," or at least the right to self-pride---sound familiar?

Thy Love Vamp had been started in 2004, put aside for a time, started sporadically over time and then, over a few days begun and completed, utilizing elements such as a somewhat "unusual: marriage, gender roles, predatory corporate raiding, and the very idea of "reality" shows. This from a story that was started as a tale depicting a love triangle, but which evolved into something more.

Sisters Yabarre! --- Believe it or not, this story (an excerpt of a soap-opera that will never be written or ended [note the closing sentence "And so the cycle continues") was influenced in large part by the 2012 Baseball World Series, specifically the San Francisco Giant's victory over the Detroit Lions (who had eliminated the Oakland Athletics that year), and by various efforts by San Francisco and San Jose to deplete Oakland of its sports teams. A soap opera parody (as I realized upon completing it), this tale involves various past and present players in the recent drama. San Francisco and San Jose were obvious enough, but I couldn't find a suitable name meaning oak (possibly if I'd gone outside the cultural box [such as in Native American culture] I might have had better luck, but for this particular tale I felt I needed to stay as "close to home" as possible), hence, the name *Kaolind* (*Kao* being oak spelled backwards; *lind* replacing the a with an i). *Yabarre* is almost an anagram for Bay Area, but with one a being replaced with a second r.

Marybel After the Genocide, a story in the style of "magical realism," was originally based on several aspects of the Gulf War (referred to here as the Genocide, which none too subtly sums up my own opinion of that war [and subsequent Middle East war efforts plus various jingoistic antics by certain politicians]. It is also loosely based on the real-life tragedy of a decorated African-American veteran of that war who was murdered soon afterwards by white joyriders, and incorporates various themes such as the legend of the people flying back to Africa, though quite a few liberties are taken with them.

Garrett Murphy is well-known in the Bay Area poetry scene as a political and human nature satirist. He lives in Oakland, CA, and has written several chapbooks of poetry and prose, *Call 9-1-1 (and Mister Punch)*, *Mother Nature Has Become a Terrorist!*, *I, Eye!*, *Now Showing*, and the novel *Yang But Yin: The Legend of Miss Dragonheel*. He has also had works published in the *Sacred Grounds Anthology*, the *New Now Now New Millennium Turn-On Anthology*, *Street Spirit*, and *At Home in the Land of the Dead*, among others.

E-Mail:

gsmurphy15@msn.com

Made in the USA
San Bernardino, CA
03 February 2016